The Funniest Kid in America

Mr. Brown

The Funniest Kid in America

GORDON KORMAN

Hyperion Paperbacks for Children
New York

Text © 2003 by Gordon Korman

Printed in the United States of America

First Hyperion Paperbacks edition, 2006
1 3 5 7 9 10 8 6 4 2
Library of Congress Cataloging-in-Publication Data on file.
ISBN 0-7868-3895-7

Visit www.hyperionbooksforchildren.com

For the Thornhill to Great Neck
Commuting Grandparents Club

Chapter 1

"You never know what will pop up in the school cafeteria. . . ."

"**W**hat's the deal with Barney? Are you telling me that, with all the crushing jaws and killer claws in the dinosaur kingdom, the only species that didn't become extinct is purple, has no teeth, and a rear end the size of a king-size water bed?"

Four-year-old Olivia Plunkett sat on a tiny chair, staring blankly up at her half brother, Max Carmody.

"And the Teletubbies. Give me a break! Are they supposed to be *real*? Hey, Tinky Winky, you've got a television growing out of your stomach! You live in a bomb shelter! Your vacuum cleaner is alive!

Whoa—heads up! There's a giant baby trapped inside the sun. . . ."

Olivia looked at him resentfully, her lower lip quivering. "Mom, he's saying mean things about Tinky Winky again!"

Max sighed. It was one of the first rules of comedy: great material can take you only so far; the rest is up to the audience. And it helps, he reflected, if the audience is old enough to understand a joke.

But just being older didn't always guarantee that an audience would be any better. Max's best friend, Maude Dolinka, was one of the smartest girls in sixth grade. She understood all the jokes. She just didn't consider them funny.

"So you think I should be laughing because there's someone in the phone book with a dumb name."

"It's hilarious!" Max argued. "Can't you picture Mr. and Mrs. Smellie naming their newborn son Irving Martin—without realizing the kid is going to be I. M. Smellie!"

"He's lucky," Maude said tragically. "You don't know what it's like to be Maude Do-stinka. Or Odd Maude the Clod. I never know what's coming next. I. M. Smellie. He's smelly. So what? He's never going to have a nickname."

Then there was Mario, Max's stepdad. He found everything that came out of Max's mouth to be absolutely hilarious. That was no help either. He'd be cracking up before Max even opened his mouth to start a joke. You couldn't tell how your routine was going over with a guy who was determined to yuk it up no matter what you said—even if you said nothing at all. It was like going by a thermometer that always gave the same temperature.

Right before he died, the famous actor Sir Donald Wolfit said, "Dying is easy; comedy is hard." Of course, how seriously could you take a "famous" actor nobody had ever heard of? And anyway, he was dead now, so it was impossible to know if he had known what he was talking about.

But it sure made sense.

Ever since Max Carmody was seven years old, his overpowering ambition was to be a professional stand-up comic. One night, congested and feverish with flu, he sat up with his mother and Mario and watched an episode of *Seinfeld*, and that was the beginning. He didn't even understand the humor. But the notion that you could be there in the bright lights, the center of attention, making everybody laugh—that would be the only life for Max.

All through elementary school, he crafted and perfected routines to be delivered to the bathroom mirror. For a long time, that was enough. The mirror thought he was a riot.

Then came the Contest.

It happened in the Bartonville Middle School cafeteria. Sydni Cox, another sixth grader, was sharing her candy bar around the table when Maude suddenly leaped to her feet with a howl of dismay.

"Oh, *no*!" This through a jam-packed mouth and immobilized tongue. "Wha's in there? Wha's in there?"

Sydni uncrumpled the wrapper and read off the ingredients: "Invert sugar, artificial flavor, corn syrup . . ."

But Maude's popping eyes were fixed on the label: CHERRY BLASTER. "Cherries!" she shrieked, her mouth open and drooling. "I can't swallow any! I'm allergic!"

The fourth person at the table, six-foot-tall yellow-blond Andrew Byrd (known for obvious reasons as Big Byrd) jumped up. In a motion that was both awkward and graceful, he hurled himself behind the much shorter Maude, grabbed her around the waist, and applied the Heimlich maneuver with the power of a pile driver.

There was a violent hiccup, and the wad of chocolate shot out of Maude's mouth, hit the bulletin board, and stuck there.

Max turned to Maude with a grin. "Thanks a lot for bringing that up."

Maude guzzled a mouthful of milk, gargled noisily, and spit it out into the garbage can. "You're a real comedian," she seethed. "I'm going to itch all over because of this! I can't even be in the same room as cherries!"

And that was when Max caught sight of it, the poster under the oozing gob of cherry chocolate.

A message that could only have been meant for him. A message that would change his life.

Chapter 2

"My vet really understands animal behavior . . . He bit me last week."

The feeling that came over Max was like nothing he'd ever experienced before. This was it— his destiny, pinpointed by a single guided missile of chocolate and saliva. He reached out a trembling hand.

Big Byrd patted Max's shoulder. "Let it go, man. The custodians will clean it up."

"Not the chocolate!" Max exclaimed, tearing off an entry form. "The poster! The contest!"

Sydni gave the poster a disinterested once-over. "You know somebody who's going to enter?"

"Me!" Max almost bellowed. "*I'm* the funniest kid in America!" There was a lot of hemming and hawing. "Oh, come on! Who do you know who's funnier than me?"

"My cousin Cyril," Big said readily. "He once went down a bobsled run on a Frisbee."

"Is he under sixteen?" Max demanded.

"I don't think so. He drives a station wagon. And he has grandkids."

"Look, Max," said Sydni kindly. "It may be that everybody laughs at your jokes around *here*. But this kind of contest is going to attract kids from all over. And some of the teenagers are bound to be better than you."

"Besides," added Maude, "you think your mom's going to let you go to Chicago? Keep dreaming."

But that evening, for the very first time, Max performed his act in front of a live audience: Olivia and two of her friends, also age four.

Nobody laughed; one of them actually cried.

"I need practice if I'm going to get good enough to win the contest!" Max groaned aloud.

"What contest?" came his mother's voice from over his shoulder.

The thing about Ellen Plunkett was that she never paid full attention to anything or anybody. She was a devoted mom, but when she talked to you, she was always doing something else at the same time—folding laundry, cooking, tidying up, or dealing with her freelance P.R. clients. It was an annoying trait, but it had its advantages. Sometimes she was so distracted that it was possible to blow something right by her.

Today was not one of those times.

"Chicago? That's four hours away!"

"But, Mom," Max pleaded. "This is my big chance! I may never get another one."

She started to load the dishwasher. "You're eleven years old, Maxie. You'll get a hundred big chances in a dozen different careers. I guarantee you're not going to be a comedian."

Okay, that was a dead end, but there was still Dad. Max would be going to his father's house tomorrow. His parents shared joint custody—"One joint one week, another joint the next," as Max put it. It was a friendly arrangement. His parents lived only a few blocks apart in the same school district. So Max could change homes on a weekly basis without too much disruption to his life.

He never went straight to his father's house. On Friday afternoons, he would go from school to the small veterinary practice Dr. Jack Carmody ran in town. There he would do his homework while his father finished up the afternoon appointments.

Max never minded the waiting. The office was a terrific place for a comedian to get ideas. Pet owners somehow seemed to be a little more colorful than ordinary people. Like Yoshi Atako, who might have been fat, but you couldn't tell, because he always had an eleven-foot python, Hector, wrapped around his torso. To Max, he looked like a walking pile of tires. Or Mrs. Kaperzinski, who was positive her parrot, Tweedle, was sick, because the bird said so. In a nifty piece of detective work, Dr. Carmody figured out that "Oh, my aching back!" was just the bird repeating what Mrs. Kaperzinski told anybody who would listen. Tweedle was fine; Mrs. Kaperzinski needed a good chiropractor.

The door to the examining room opened, and out stepped Dr. Carmody, escorting Mrs. Kaperzinski and Tweedle.

"It's impossible for a bird to have carpal tunnel syndrome," the vet was explaining to Mrs. K. "If you stop talking about your wrist, he won't hear it, and he won't say it."

He turned to his son. "Max, have you been doing your comedy routine in the waiting room?"

Max was surprised. "What makes you say that?"

Tweedle squawked. "Aaak! What's the deal with librarians?"

Max looked sheepish. "I need to perform for an audience, Dad. Mom signed me up for this comedy contest in Chicago, and I have to get my act in shape." It would be easier to get Dad on board if he thought Mom was already a yes.

Dr. Carmody was dubious. "Your mother's taking you to Chicago?"

"It's a national contest," Max went on. "Kids are coming from all over to do stand-up. First prize is a thousand bucks and a guest spot on *Comedy Planet*. What a break that would be!"

"Well, I have to assume Mom knows what she's doing," Dr. Carmody mused skeptically.

Perfect, thought Max. Dad was a go. That left just Mom. She was a hard case, but she had an Achilles' heel.

Back with Mom and Olivia the next week, Max waited until Mario called in from the road.

Mario Plunkett was a long-distance truck driver. Max called him "the biggest load of rotting cabbages on eighteen wheels." Mario phoned every night to check in with his wife and sing Olivia her bedtime song. He always asked to speak to Max too, which kind of drove Max crazy. Mario was Olivia's dad, not his.

Besides, the guy was so boring! The calls were a never-ending travelogue of places he passed on his routes: milestones, hometowns of celebrities, the anchovy capital of the Midwest, the world's largest Easter egg.

"Guess what?" Mom exclaimed, trying to share the earpiece with her daughter. "Daddy's calling from Coldwater, Ohio, where the manure spreader was invented!"

Max usually made a point of refusing to take the phone, out of loyalty to his Dad.

Ellen Plunkett was adept at covering up. "Not tonight, dear. Max is upstairs doing his homework. . . ."

"I'll say hi," Max volunteered, grabbing the receiver. "How's it going, Mario? What was for dinner tonight? Roadkill again?"

Mario laughed his head off, which he would have done even if Max had given him a weather report. Finally, he managed, "So how are you, kiddo? Did you have a good week with your old man?" Mario never missed a chance to ask about Dr. Carmody, which almost made Max feel guilty about disliking the guy.

"Pretty good." Max dropped his voice so his mother, who had returned to some paperwork, wouldn't hear. "Dad's going to take me to Chicago so I can enter this comedy contest for kids."

"That's fantastic, Max!" Mario exclaimed. "You're going to knock 'em dead! Any chance Mom, Livy, and I could go too? Man, it would be great to watch you on a real stage!"

"To be honest," Max said carefully, "Mom wasn't thrilled with the idea when I first told her about it."

"You let me talk to her," his stepfather promised. "This is important! It could be your big chance!"

Max grimaced. He should have been smiling; Mario never let him down. But accepting favors from him always made Max feel a little unfaithful to his Dad.

"Hey," said Mario. "The Voles have a big home stand coming up. What do you say—let's try to catch a game."

The Tri-County Voles were Bartonville's ice-hockey team. They played in some subbasement minor league and still managed to own last place despite pathetic competition. A season-ticket holder and number-one fan, Mario was always bugging Max to go with him.

"I don't know," mumbled Max. "Middle school is pretty tough. Major homework."

"There's a Thursday night matchup with the Centerville Storm," Mario wheedled. "It should be a dogfight!"

"I'm not really into hockey," Max said lamely.

It was a lie. The truth was that if Jack Carmody had wanted to take him to see the Voles, Max would have put up with the clumsy play, the uncomfortable bleachers, and the ancient Zamboni that filled the rink with smoke every time it came out to clean the ice.

One thing about Mario: he was always gracious in defeat. "We'll do it another time."

"I should probably get going," Max began.

"Tell me a joke first."

"Aw, Mario, I don't feel like it."

"Come on. I miss you guys."

Max sighed. "Did you hear about the sewer cleaner who put Odor-Eaters in his shoes? He took one step and disappeared."

Mario howled.

Chapter 3

"You've got to love stage names. It may say Dorkmeister Doofus on your birth certificate, but to the public, you're Johnny Lightning."

Max agonized over the application. It would be just his luck to miss out on the greatest chance ever because he skipped a line, or forgot to dot an *i* or cross a *t*. Everything had to be perfect.

Carefully, he block printed his contact information—cursive was out of the question. He gave the address of his father's veterinary practice, since SUITE 1H had a very professional sound to it. Maybe they'd think it belonged to a high-powered agent with an eye for young talent. For *Name*, on a whim he put MAX COMEDY.

He sat back and looked at it. It appealed to him. A lot of the great performers had stage names. He frowned critically. It was missing something. He took his pen and added another *x* on the end of MAX.

"Max Carmody" was just some kid from Bartonville, Ohio. But MAXX COMEDY looked like a rising star!

There was only one thing left to do for this application, and it was a biggie. Max had to submit a three-minute videotape or DVD of his act. After viewing all the auditions, the judges would decide which thirty finalists would be given performance slots at the Balsam Auditorium on November sixteenth.

"Big, your folks have a video camera, right?" he said the next day before homeroom.

Big Byrd took an instant shine to the idea. "I'll be the director," he decided. "Maude, you can executive produce, and we'll get Sydni to handle casting—"

"*I'm* the cast," Max interrupted. "It's just me doing my act."

An agitated low whistling sound began to emanate from Big's nose. A few years ago, the tall boy had undergone an operation to correct chronic respiratory infections. He still had tubes in his sinus

16

canals, which he could sometimes play like a built-in kazoo.

"I don't know if I can work under these conditions," he told Max anxiously. "I don't want to get involved in a low-budget project."

"You won't," Max assured him, "because this is a *no*-budget project." He turned to Maude. "How about you?"

"Do you need a steady hand for that?" Maude asked nervously.

"Oh, no," Max said sarcastically. "It's much better when the camera's shaking all over the place and you can't tell what's going on!"

The three glanced up as Sydni came running down the hall, her face shining with excitement.

"Guys! Guys! Guess what? You are looking at the new assistant refreshments chairperson for the student council!"

This was a big deal for Sydni, who had been student president of their elementary class. She was having trouble getting used to being a nobody as a sixth grader in middle school.

"It's over," Maude predicted. "You'll drop us like a hot potato if you ever fall in with that crowd."

"It doesn't work that way," Sydni insisted. "You

know how the president of the United States gets to take all his loser friends and give them cushy jobs in the White House? Well, it's the same in middle school. You guys could end up popular because of me."

"Those student-council types would never accept us," Maude said flatly.

"They just don't know you yet," Sydni argued. "Look at Big. A lot of kids think he's a nutcase, but deep down . . ."

Her voice trailed off. Big had formed a rectangular camera frame with his thumbs and forefingers, and was scanning the hallway, "filming" the students who passed by. The strains of "Hooray for Hollywood" tooted through his nasal tubes.

"Listen," she began again, "I couldn't get elected dogcatcher at this school. So I have to make the right connections. Do you know who the *chief* refreshments person is? Only Amanda Locke, that's who!"

Maude was instantly alert. "Isn't that Madison Locke's younger sister?"

"Exactly!" exclaimed Sydni. "Madison was student council president last year. She's in high school now."

Maude's jaw stiffened like the scoop of a power

shovel. "Madison Locke! Do you know what she had the classlessness to say to me?"

"When did you ever talk to Madison Locke?" asked Big.

"Four years ago," Maude shot back. "I was standing by the jungle gym in the playground at elementary school, and she walked by and said, 'Nice pants.' Just like that!"

"Maybe she liked your pants," Max suggested.

"She said it with disdain," Maude insisted. "She said it like I don't know how to dress."

"You were seven years old!" Max argued impatiently. "I'll bet you didn't know how to tie your shoes, either!"

"Ever since that day," Maude continued bitterly, "my life has been a procession of snobs who treat me like snail slime. And don't think I'll ever forget that it all started with Madison Locke!"

Sydni cast her a scornful look. "You're weird."

"This isn't getting my video made," Max complained. "The deadline is in two weeks."

Big ran a hand through his scarecrow-yellow hair. "I don't know if I can deal with this time pressure."

Max blew his stack. "It's a three-minute video,

not *The Lord of the Rings*! You just point the camera. I'll do the rest."

". . . So you have to ask yourself: is it that all gym teachers naturally grow whistles around their necks? Or is it that all whistles somehow grow gym teachers?

"Thank you, ladies and gentlemen. You've been a fantastic audience! Good night!"

Max pressed the pause button on the Plunketts' VCR. The image froze. "What do you think? It's funny enough, right?"

Sydni shrugged. "I guess so. It seemed to be sort of kind of okay."

Big helped himself to a handful of Mrs. Plunkett's cookies. "I'll put a powerful spotlight behind you next time. You'll look like Hercules!"

"I don't want to look like Hercules," Max complained. "I want to look like Jay Leno doing his monologue."

"It didn't come out like that," said Sydni thoughtfully.

Maude snapped her fingers. "You know what's missing?"

"Flash bombs!" put in Big. "Every time you tell a joke, *boom*!"

"There's no laughing," Maude went on. "Here's all this stuff that's supposed to be funny, but nobody's laughing."

"Of course nobody's laughing!" Max exploded. "Nobody's there! There was no audience when we shot it!"

"I was there," said Maude. "What am I—chopped liver?"

"You're only one person," Max retorted. "And besides, you never laugh, because you take all the jokes too personally."

Maude bristled. "How can I laugh at gym teachers? Every gym teacher I've ever had hated me. You know why? Because I *think*. I ask questions like, Why do they call it *dribbling*? If I had spaghetti sauce running down my chin, would I call it *bouncing*?"

Max frowned. "I see what you guys mean. Without audience reaction, the rhythm is off. But where am I going to find an audience? I can't send in a whole tape of Teletubby jokes in front of Olivia and the diaper squad. Besides, they don't laugh."

The quest began to reshoot the tape in front of a crowd.

At school, the only teacher willing to volunteer his whole class as guinea pigs was Mr. Mancuso, who presided over in-school suspension. Max performed his routine for as tough a group of hard cases as any prison would have been able to come up with. They didn't laugh. In fact, they threw things. One of them shook down Maude for her lunch money.

"Stand up to him!" Sydni urged. "We can take that guy!"

"Oh, sure," said Maude. "He's a foot taller than me. I can't even see his head from down here." Maude was short and squat, with a perpetually aggrieved expression.

In the end, Sydni faced down the burly eighth grader alone. Brashly, she ordered him to "hand over that money or suffer the consequences!"

He just laughed. "Says who?"

"The President's Council on In-School Civility," she said evenly. "It's a commission set up by the federal government to investigate bullying in public schools."

Big was in awe as his friend strode away, the bills clutched tightly in her fist.

"Sydni, that was amazing! How did you find out about the President's Council on In-School Civility?"

"Just keep walking," she muttered through

clenched teeth. "And pray he doesn't look it up on the Internet."

The Bartonville Seniors Center provided a willing, but not very able, audience for Max. There were a few polite chuckles, and a scattering of applause, and hardly anyone walked out of the lounge where the performance took place. But most of the jokes were drowned out by one man in the back row, whose foghorn voice kept repeating, "What did he say? What did he say?"

Every day after school, Max, Maude, Sydni, and Big prowled the streets of Bartonville in search of a group of people who needed a good laugh. Max accepted without question that his three friends would be there to support him, even though they all thought his idea made no sense. The four were so completely different that each one's interests seemed almost alien to the other three. Yet they always showed up, even Maude, who complained every inch of the way.

No one was in much of a mood for comedy while waiting in line to pay traffic tickets at the county courthouse. At the supermarket, shoppers hid their faces behind magazines, and ignored Max as if he were doing something shameful.

They did better at the library, until Max was shushed halfway through his routine. A command performance at the firehouse might have been a success if it hadn't been for a comedy-hating Dalmatian. And the manager at the local bank called the police, and had Max and his crew escorted from the building.

"Hey, officer," said Big conversationally, "how full is your jail? You think any of the prisoners like comedy?"

They let him off with a warning.

Max was getting panicky. "What kind of a sad-sack town *is* this? Nobody wants to laugh!"

Big had another idea. "What if we shoot you doing your act to a brick wall? Get it? Talk to the wall?"

"Only if the wall is going to laugh at my jokes!" growled Max. "What am I going to do? The deadline is practically a week away!"

"We'll keep trying," Maude promised.

"Count me out," said Sydni seriously. "I've got my first job for the refreshment committee this weekend. It's the annual student council–PTA joint meeting, where they plan events for the whole year. You guys promised to help, remember?"

"Now, wait a minute," said Max. "I'm in the middle of getting ready for the biggest thing that's ever happened to me. No way would I volunteer to push brownies at the student council."

"Well, okay, so you didn't," Sydni admitted. "But I *need* you guys! It's at Amanda Locke's place. She lives in that huge old farmhouse outside of town. I can't handle it all by myself."

"Is Madison going to be there?" Maude asked tensely.

Sydni turned on her. "Maude Dolinka, if you embarrass me in front of the student council, there won't be enough left of you to fill up a doggie bag!"

"Do you want my help or don't you?" she shot right back.

"I know!" said Big. "We'll put hidden messages on the tape—you know, stuff like 'This would be a heck of a lot funnier if there was an audience.'"

Max put his hands over his ears. He could see the deadline hurtling toward him like a comet.

How was he *ever* going to get his entry done?

Chapter 4

"Why do they call it writer's block? Do trash collectors get garbage block?"

I go to school in a classroom where everything is laminated. The signs are laminated. The posters are laminated. Our work folders are laminated. Our teacher is a compulsive laminator. . . .

Max was in his room at Chateau East, Mom and Mario's house, hunched over his comedy note-book. Whenever he was tense, or worried, or unhappy, it helped him feel better to work on new material for his act. Some of his funniest jokes came out of his worst moods. And right now he was feeling pretty low.

I always wonder what her house looks like.
The roof doesn't leak because it's laminated.
Inside are laminated chairs and laminated
plants. . . .

No, he thought. Not funny enough.

There's a laminated poodle wondering why
it's so hard to drink out of a laminated water
dish. . . .

Better, but . . .

He didn't need this new bit. He had plenty of material. What he needed was a good tape to send in to the contest. Why was it so impossible to find an audience? People should be grateful someone wanted to entertain them!

Calm down, he told himself. If worse came to worst, he could always send in the first tape, the one with no audience at all. That was the freshest, before he'd done the same jokes twenty-five times in one week. But deep down he knew that if he wasn't picked for the contest, he would never forgive himself for not finding a way to get it exactly right.

He forced his mind to concentrate on the notebook.

If I'm ever walking around town, and I run into a man who's completely encased in plastic, I'll say, "Hi, Mr. Jones. Your wife's a great teacher. By the way, do you have to poke airholes in that?"

A burst of high-pitched giggles reached him from the next room. That was Olivia and her friends, playing in her bedroom. Didn't it figure? They were too young to understand Max's humor. But let one of them accidentally rip off Barbie's head, and they were rolling on the floor.

It was too bad, he reflected wanly. That laugh had come right at the end of his laminating joke. The timing had been so perfect he almost felt like taking a bow. If only there were laughs like that on his audition tape!

When the solution came to him, it was the simplest thing in the world. He didn't have to do his act in front of an audience for this tape! All he needed was laughter—*any* laughter! Then, after every joke, he'd edit in the audience reaction, and it would sound just like the people were responding to his routine. TV shows did it all the time. When the studio audience didn't laugh enough, the engineers used a computer to add in some canned laughs. Well, this was exactly the same thing.

He grabbed his pocket cassette recorder, and headed downstairs to the den. For the next half hour, he channel-surfed from sitcom to sitcom, taping snickers, giggles, belly laughs, and outright screams.

Listening to it was a real disappointment. The problem was, since all these snippets came from real shows, it was impossible to get rid of little bits of talking and music amid the laughter. It would be a dead giveaway if, on his audition tape, the judges suddenly heard a split second of dialogue or theme music from *Friends* or *Everybody Loves Raymond*. If they found out he'd used fake laughter, no way would he get picked as a contestant!

No, he was going to have to record some *real* people laughing. But where could he find enough of them, all in one place, to sound like an audience?

The telephone rang. Sydni. The stress of the upcoming student council/PTA joint session was clearly evident in her voice. "Okay, okay. Maude says she'll buy the drinks and pick up the cookies

29

from the bakery. And Big's volunteered to help me set up the tables and chairs. I think I've got it under control, but I need one more helper to make sure everything's perfect. Come on, Max, what do you say?"

Max's eyes narrowed. "How many people are you expecting?"

"About fifty."

For the first time since his troubles with the videotape had begun, Max allowed himself the luxury of a smile.

"Count me in, Syd," he promised. "What are friends for?"

Chapter 5

"Refreshments.
What a strange word.
How does stuffing your
face make you feel
'refreshed'?"

Max was due to make the switchover to his father's custody right after school that Friday. But Dr. Carmody had shut down his office and gone to an emergency at the Plandome farm, where Madonna, a prize Guernsey cow, was ready to calve at any second. So Ellen Plunkett became Max's chauffeur out to the Locke house for the student council–PTA joint session.

They stopped to pick up Big Byrd on the way. In the backseat, Max unzipped the pocket of his jacket to reveal his mini tape recorder hidden there.

Big was confused. "If you get caught playing music at this thing, Sydni's going to freak!"

"Not music," Max replied in a low voice. "I'm going to record people laughing. Then I'll dub it onto our video, and it'll sound just like there's an audience responding to my jokes."

The plan drew a honk of admiration from the tube in Big's left sinus. "You're a genius!" he exclaimed. "Don't worry, Max. I'll get them to laugh for you."

"No," Max said quickly. "It has to sound totally natural. With fifty people in the same room, there's bound to be some laughing sometime. Just let it happen."

The Lockes lived in a sprawling converted farmhouse just outside the town limits. Sydni was pacing the wraparound porch when the Plunkett car pulled up the drive.

She rushed over to meet Max and Big. "No one is helping me," she complained. "Not even Amanda, and it's *her* job!"

"Max, don't forget your suitcase," called Mrs. Plunkett. "And remember, your father's coming for you at nine."

"Okay, Mom. Thanks for the lift."

As Mrs. Plunkett drove off, Sydni looked nervously at Max's duffle. "Don't let Amanda see that. She'll think you're here for a slumber party." She took a deep breath. "Calm down, Sydni," she said to herself. "Everything's going to be fine. You've given it your all. There's nothing more you can do."

"Praying wouldn't hurt," Big put in helpfully.

She scowled at him. "Where's Maude?"

As if on cue, Mr. Dolinka's van pulled up the gravel driveway, and out hopped Maude. The round-faced girl carried a large shopping bag in each hand.

"Thanks, Dad. I'll catch a ride home with Max."

She shut the door, and the van pulled away.

"No!" shrieked Sydni. "Wait! Maude, you forgot to unload the rest of the stuff!"

Maude shrugged. "I've got everything right here."

The eyes very nearly popped out of Sydni's head. "There should be a dozen large boxes from the bakery! And what about the drinks?"

Maude set her packages down, and opened them to reveal their contents. One held a gallon jug of grape drink; the other, a five-pound paper sack of cookies.

"That's it?" she howled. "We've got fifty people coming! Maude Dolinka, where is the food I sent you for?"

"I couldn't get it," she replied defensively. "There wasn't enough money."

"I gave you a hundred-dollar bill!"

"Well, the pants alone cost eighty-five," Maude explained reasonably.

Max stared at his best friend. Maude was sporting skintight black leather pants with a rattlesnake pattern on the pockets and cuffs, and hand-tooled bands of cactus plants down the outer seams.

"Oooh," said Big. "Those are nice."

"I must be losing my mind!" shrilled Sydni. "I told you to pick up the refreshments! Nobody said anything about buying pants!"

Maude drew herself up to her full height, which was about three-quarters of Big's. "Madison Locke," she said evenly, "thinks I don't know how to dress. Well, wait till she sees me tonight."

"She isn't even here!" moaned Sydni.

"Good thing too," added Max, "because we definitely don't have enough food for her."

"She'll be here eventually," said Maude stubbornly. "And I'm not leaving until she sees me wearing the most expensive pants in the entire Bartonville Mall. Believe me, I checked every store."

"And did you check for sizes?" Max inquired. "You look like ten pounds of sausage stuffed into a five-pound bag."

"This is insane, even for you, Maude Dolinka!" raged Sydni. "You bought these pants with stolen money!"

"Not stolen," Maude explained. "Borrowed. Tomorrow morning I'll go back to the mall and return them for a full refund. And the student council ends up eighty-five bucks ahead of where they'd be if I blew it all on junk. You'll be a hero."

"I'll be lynched," Sydni predicted mournfully. "Let's get in the kitchen and see what we can make of this disaster!"

Just how big a disaster became apparent when the packages were opened.

"Artificially Flavored, Artificially Colored Grape Drink Product" read the label on the jug. On the bag was printed "Broken and/or Slightly Irregular Chocolate Chip Cookies—5 lbs."

"Broken cookies? We're going to serve the PTA and the student council *broken cookies*?"

"They're going to get broken eventually when you put them in your mouth," Maude reasoned. "So look at these as *pre*-broken."

"And how are we going to serve the drinks?" Sydni demanded. "With an eyedropper?"

Big pulled a large punch bowl from a lower cupboard. "We're going to have to improvise," he decided. He opened the refrigerator. "Jackpot!" A carton of orange juice appeared, along with a half-full quart of Gatorade. Both went into the punch bowl, followed by the gallon of grape drink.

"Empty all the ice-cube trays," advised Max. "That'll make it look fuller."

Next they added varying amounts of root beer, lemonade, ginger ale, and iced tea. They filled the bowl up the rest of the way with water, and topped it off with three pints of Häagen-Dazs ice cream.

"See?" said Big proudly. "It's a float!"

"It looks like Love Canal," observed Max.

"What would you call that color?" mused Maude. "A kind of grayish brownish purple—"

Amanda appeared in the kitchen doorway. "How's it going in here?"

"Great!" chorused the four.

The doorbell rang. The guests had begun to arrive.

The meeting was held in the huge double parlor of the elegant old house. It lasted almost an hour. And by the time the president of the PTA brought it to a close, Max, leaning in from the kitchen, was starting to worry. The PTA and the student council were probably the most boring groups of people on the face of the earth, and the topics of discussion could not have been more unfunny: the scheduling of school dances; the lunchroom committee; the Red Cross blood drive; who would be in charge of buying the trophies for the chess club. He had not recorded a single inch of tape. There hadn't been a weak smile, let alone a laugh.

"Don't worry," Big whispered. "By the end of the night, this'll be a party."

"It's hard to party on swamp water and cookie dust," Max reminded him grimly. "Don't be surprised if they make an early night of it."

Sydni wheeled in the punch bowl with a look on her face that said she was marching to her own execution. Max felt for her, but he couldn't worry about that now. If he didn't get his laugh track tonight, chances were he'd never get one before the deadline. Strolling nonchalantly, he circulated among the guests, hand in his pocket, trigger finger on the RECORD button of his tape machine.

Laugh, he thought morosely. *Come on, laugh.*

The only reaction was a stir of conversation around the punch bowl.

"Now, that's an interesting flavor."

"Kind of a chocolate licorice purple—"

"I hope it tastes better than it looks."

Big waded into the crowd, flashed Max a thumbs-up, and announced loudly, "Hey, did you hear about the farmer's daughter and the giant panda that escaped from the zoo?"

A few heads turned politely in his direction.

Big looked completely blank for a moment, then threw his head back and filled the room with loud laughter.

"Yeah!" he cackled. "That's a good one!"

Maude marched up to Max, moving stiffly in her tight pants. "I've been listening in on conversations," she intoned. "The cookies are a hit."

"You heard wrong," Max replied. "What they said was 'Something hit the cookies.' Like a train."

She looked at her watch. "I hope Madison gets here soon. When the food's all gone, people are going to start to leave."

"In that case, you've got nothing to worry about," Max informed her. "That punch is going to be here through the next Ice Age."

"Hey, did you hear about the Russian ballerina and the mutant hippo with the two hundred I.Q.?" piped up Big's voice from across the room. Another hearty laugh, his alone.

Sydni sidled up to Max and Maude. "What's the matter with Big? Why's he yelling half-jokes and hee-hawing in people's faces?"

"It's a long story," sighed Max, "and a really sad one."

"When's your Dad coming, Max? I've got to be out of here before Amanda finds me! This is the worst night of my life!"

"He'll be here soon," Max promised. "He said nine, but he's always early."

What a disaster this night had turned out to be! And it had nothing to do with poisoned punch and broken cookies. Of all the places to come for a laugh track! A house full of zombies.

A manicured hand reached out and grasped Sydni's shoulder from behind. "There you are, Sydni."

"Am-amanda!" Sydni stammered. "Hi! Great meeting. When you guys voted to have the flagpole power-washed, I got goose bumps."

"You've put in a lot of work tonight," Amanda

cooed. "Here, I've brought you a glass of punch."
And she held out a brimming cupful of black sludge,
her eyes daring Sydni to turn it down.

"Gee, thanks," Sydni managed. "But I'm not very
thirsty. And I should go and see if the cookie platter
is getting low—"

"It's not," Amanda told her flatly. "Now, drink."

Hands shaking, Sydni brought the plastic cup to
her lips.

"Did you hear about the computer programmer
and the man-eating plant? Ha-ha-ha!"

It was unreal, Max thought—being in this situation, in this strange house, watching one of your
closest friends drink a cup of toxic waste.

"Delicious," said Sydni.

"You didn't taste it yet," snarled Amanda.

"Yes, I did."

"No, you didn't!" Amanda reached out her hand
and pushed the cup up, tilting it right into Sydni's
face. The black drink slopped down her chin, and all
across the front of her white blouse. The cup hit the
floor with a splat. A few drops of punch splashed
onto the rattlesnake pattern on the left cuff of
Maude's leather pants.

"Oh, *no*!" Maude grabbed a napkin from the

serving table, and bent over to scrub at the leather.

R-R-RIP!

The entire seat of her pants split up the middle and opened like a rose.

Chapter 6

"_Underwear._ That word is always good for a cheap laugh. . . ."

It's possible that the incident would have passed unnoticed if it hadn't been for the scream of anguish that was torn from Maude's throat.

For a moment, there was dead silence in the double parlor as fifty pairs of eyes focused on Maude Dolinka's underwear. And then the entire student council and PTA of Bartonville Middle School dissolved into wild raucous laughter.

It happened so fast that Max almost missed it. But he scrambled to get his hand in his pocket and hit RECORD.

It was a bigger laugh than he ever could have hoped for—wave after wave of rollicking mirth. The front-row audience at Comic Relief could not have provided a better laugh track.

Face flaming red, Maude began to back toward the front door. Max, Sydni, and Big followed her.

"Get out of my house!" raged Amanda. "You'll never work for the student council again!"

Sydni looked even more upset than Maude.

Big waved to the crowd. "Did you get that, Max? They *loved* my jokes! Maybe *I'm* the funniest kid in America!"

Madison Locke was coming up her porch steps when the front door opened and Maude backed out. At the sound of the ninth grader's footsteps, Maude wheeled, and stood frozen there, face-to-face with her nemesis of four years before.

Madison looked her up and down with no sign of recognition, and walked past her into the house, tossing over her shoulder, "Nice pants."

"You're lucky," said Big with deep respect. "Madison Locke talked to you *twice*."

The kitchen window opened. "And don't come back!"

Out flew Max's duffel bag, unzipped and strewing clothes all over the bushes.

A horn honked, and Dr. Carmody's Volvo wagon pulled up the drive. With the help of his three friends, Max gathered up his things.

Maude started to comment, but Sydni cut her off. "Don't you dare open your mouth, Maude Dolinka! You're not allowed to say anything for the rest of your life! You can't return those pants now! They're ruined! The student council's never going to get its money back!"

"What do you care?" mumbled Maude. "You don't work for them anymore."

Once in his seat belt, Max rewound his tape and hit PLAY. The car filled with rich, full laughter. "Perfect," he said with satisfaction.

"Turn it off," moaned Maude.

Dr. Carmody's car phone rang sharply. He answered, listened briefly, and jammed on the brakes. "Be right there!" A quick U-turn had them speeding away from town. "We have to make a little detour to Plandome Farm."

"I thought that was this afternoon," said Max.

His father laughed. "Madonna couldn't be hurried. She's having her calf in her own sweet time, and that's right now. Sorry, kids, but it's an emergency."

The Plandome property was a small, prosperous dairy farm about five miles east of Bartonville, at the end of a dirt road. Dr. Carmody parked near the wood-frame house, grabbed his black bag and a suit of coveralls, and ran for the barn.

Max and the others got out and stood around the car.

"This is just great!" Maude complained. "It's the perfect time to be visiting strangers—when my pants are torn and my caboose is on the loose!"

An eruption of loud mooing came from the barn.

"We should go in there and check it out," said Big. "It's the miracle of life."

"It's the miracle of *gross*," Sydni amended. "How long does it take to have a cow? When are we going home?"

The corrals and paddocks near the barn were empty. All the animals were inside for the night— with one exception. In a small sturdy pen stood a lone Guernsey bull. He was quiet and motionless, but he never took his eyes off them.

"I'll bet that's the father," said Big excitedly. "Hang in there, dude. You're going to be a daddy soon!"

"Don't get him mad," joked Max. "He's already pretty riled because Maude's wearing his brother."

"You think I'm afraid of him?" said Maude scornfully. "My whole life is about taking bull." She picked up a clod of dry earth, and threw it at the pen. It rattled the narrow gate, knocking the padlock clean off.

"You crazy idiot!" Max hissed. "Now he's loose!"

"He's just standing there," observed Big.

"I'm going in the barn," said Sydni. "At least it's safe."

All four walked hurriedly to the barn. The bull made no move to leave his pen.

Inside, the scene could not have been wilder. The farmer and two hired men strained to hold the cow down, while Dr. Carmody's arms delved deep inside the animal. For Madonna's part, she was yelling her head off—loud, frantic *moos*—while trying to kick at the vet. An overpowering barnyard smell hung in the air like a fog.

All four stood in awe, watching the birth. Max had heard his father describing this many times. But the reality surpassed anything he could have imagined. He knew that all was proceeding normally, that his father was a trained professional. But to hear the animal's tortured complaints, to watch the struggle—and right in the middle of it, Dad—was a frightening experience.

He jammed his hands into his pockets, mostly to try to control their trembling. So uptight was he that he failed to notice his clenched knuckle pushing in the RECORD button on his mini tape machine.

Five agonizing minutes later, the calf was born. Covered in gore, it stood before them on trembling legs.

Big was overcome with emotion. He rushed forward and embraced the newborn creature.

POW!

Madonna's hind leg shot out like a piston, catching Big full on the shoulder. One second he was hugging the calf; the next, he was airborne, landing in a heap in the soft hay that covered the floor.

"Big!" Max, Maude, and Sydni rushed to the aid of their dazed friend.

"I'm okay, I'm okay!" Big assured them.

By the time they hauled him back to his feet, all four were covered in the same gunk as the new baby.

"Look at my beautiful eighty-five-dollar pants!" Maude lamented.

"The way I see it," said Sydni stiffly, "they're the student council's pants. And they aren't worth eighty-five *cents* now!"

All that remained was for the newcomer to be named. Farmer Plandome liked Maude's suggestion the best: Madison.

It was as the weary party climbed back into the Volvo that Maude noticed the bullpen. It was empty.

"Where's the bull?" she rasped.

Dr. Carmody saw it first—in the rearview mirror, coming up fast. He stomped on the gas so hard that the wagon's tires spun on the dirt road.

Max tossed a terrified glance over his shoulder. "Hurry, Dad! He's right behind us!"

"We named her Madison!" Big called out the window.

Finally, the tire treads gained traction, and the Volvo roared forward. But by this time, the bull was at top speed. He continued to close the gap.

"Oh, this is bad!" moaned Maude. "Even for me!"

The bull was within inches of the back bumper when the Volvo's turbo kicked in. Max watched as they left the enraged animal far behind.

Dr. Carmody pulled out his cell phone and began dialing the farmhouse. "It's not like Roy Plandome to leave the pen unsecured. What was he thinking?"

In Max's jacket pocket, the tape reached the end, stopped with a tiny click, and began to rewind automatically.

Chapter 7

"When you can't find something, it's like _Star Trek_ came and beamed it into outer space. . . ."

Dad's house, Chateau West, was exactly four blocks west of Chateau East, along the same meandering tree-lined street, Oak Drive. The next morning, Max awoke there, gasping for breath, with Dudley, the "canine alarm clock," parked over his nose and mouth. Dr. Carmody's considerable skill with animals did not extend to the obedience training of his own pet. Dudley did what he pleased, and that included waking people up by suffocation.

Choking and spitting, Max threw the dog off and ran downstairs. Today was the day. He would dub the laugh track onto the video of his routine, transfer it to a DVD, and send it and his application to contest headquarters in Chicago. The first step on the stairway to stardom? Perhaps.

He rushed to the coat rack in the front hall.

And froze.

His jacket, with the mini tape machine in the zipper pocket, was *gone*!

"Dad!"

Then he saw the note on the hall table. It was in Jack Carmody's unmistakable scribbled hand:

MAX—

SOME NIGHT, HUH?. TOOK YOUR JACKET TO THE CLEANERS (WHAT A MESS!). THERE'S CEREAL IN THE CABINET, BUT BE CAREFUL NOT TO GET ANY ON THE FLOOR. BRAN GIVES DUDLEY GAS. BACK SOON.

DAD

"No-o-o!"

Dudley looked on in mild interest through the slats in the banister as Max dashed for first the yellow pages and then the phone.

"Hi, this is Max Carmody. My father just dropped off a blue windbreaker. In the right zipper pocket there should be a tape recorder."

"I'll check." A moment later, the voice came back on the line. "I've got the jacket, but there's nothing in any of the pockets."

Max felt his heart lurch. "Are you sure? It's a matter of life and death."

"Sorry, honey. I searched the whole bin."

Oh, great! The only good thing to come out of last night's disaster was his laugh track. And now that was gone. October 12—the deadline for the contest—was only a week away. He needed to get his entry in the mail on Wednesday to make sure it got there.

Wednesday passed with no sign of the missing tape recorder. Friday loomed, the Express Mail deadline. An overnight package would still arrive in Chicago in time.

"Forget the laugh track. Send it now," urged Maude, who wasn't really fond of the source of the canned laughter.

"Sure, why not?" Sydni agreed listlessly. "I'm ruined, but there's still a chance for you."

"Don't forget, it's my directorial debut," Big put in. He had taken to wearing collared shirts spread open with a bright red imitation-silk ascot underneath. Big thought it made him look like a filmmaker. In reality, the sight of a six-foot-tall sixth grader stalking through the school halls in an ascot, toot-tootling "Scotland the Brave" through his sinus tubes was more amazing than anything he might have recorded on videotape.

"There's still one last deadline," Max insisted. "Mario knows a FedEx driver who does the late deliveries in Chicago. Mario can leave tomorrow and rendezvous with this guy outside Piqua. He'll get my entry to contest headquarters by five."

"Why can't I have a great stepfather like that?" Maude complained. "My parents should get divorced."

Life at Chateau East when Mario was home was like *The Simpsons* minus the funny parts. If there was an annoying habit Mario Plunkett *didn't* have, Max hadn't heard of it yet. He parked the cab of his eighteen-wheeler in the narrow driveway, effectively sealing off the garage. He hummed classic rock songs from the 1970s. He filled in crossword puzzles with made-up words like RALGE and CLEAPOD. He talked to the characters on TV.

The only thing more irritating than Mario was Mario and Mom together. The Plunketts were an affectionate couple, constantly stealing kisses, holding hands, and sitting in each other's lap. Mario would surprise his wife with "thoughtful" little gifts. But since they came from Mario, they were always stupid souvenirs from his travels, like an anklet where every link was in the shape of the Spindle-Top oil gusher in Texas.

"Who wears jewelry on their feet, anyway?" Max complained.

"*I* do," Sydni told him over the phone. "And so do most girls."

"Really?" Their group of friends was so tight that Max and Big rarely thought of Sydni and Maude as female. Despite the huge amounts of time the four spent together, Max never noticed where the two girls wore their jewelry, or if they wore any at all.

"Look," Sydni explained reasonably. "Your mom and Mario are separated a lot because of his job. So they're lovey-dovey when they're together. So what? Look on the bright side. Your mom could have married a real jerk. Mario's a great guy. *Maude* likes him, and she hates everybody."

"She doesn't have to live with him," Max grumbled.

Lately, Mario had become a walking play-by-play announcement of the Tri-County Voles' 1–0 overtime loss to the Bucyrus Blowfish. He either would not or could not shut up about it.

"You should have been there, Max. With three seconds left in regulation time, Hazeltine had a breakaway and faked the goalie out of his jockstrap."

"What happened?" asked his wife.

"He stepped on the puck," Mario admitted. "Broke his leg in three places. I can't believe you missed it."

"Next time," said Max. Next time the moon fell out of the sky.

And it didn't help his mood that, on Saturday morning, the sad news came from the dry cleaners. The mini tape recorder was still nowhere to be found, and this was definitely the final deadline. Mario was packing his bag for the next big haul— three hundred bushels of eggplants headed for North Dakota.

As Max stuffed his audition video, with no laugh track, into a padded envelope, he recalled a poem his class had read late the year before:

For of all sad words
of tongue or pen,
The saddest are these:
"It might have been!"

Okay, it was a dumb poem that didn't even rhyme right. But whoever wrote it understood exactly how Max felt.

The doorbell rang, and a moment later he heard Mario's voice. "Jack, what a surprise."

Max flew down the stairs to find his father standing in the doorway, holding the mini tape recorder. "It was in my laundry bag the whole time," Dr. Carmody explained. "It must have fallen out of the pocket before I went to the cleaners."

Mario looked at his watch. "If I'm going to catch Barry in Piqua, I've got to leave, like, *now*."

Max snatched the machine from his father's hand. "Ten minutes!" he cried, sprinting for the den.

He booted up the iMac and popped the cassette into the tape player. He had already transferred the three-minute video onto a disk. Mario had blown the iMac's speakers downloading Led Zeppelin from the Internet, so Max could see the performance on the monitor, but he couldn't hear it. This was no problem. His act was like second nature by now. He followed along by reading his lips and body language. Carefully, he identified his punch lines. Those were the spots where he needed big audience reaction.

Working with the laugh track was a stickier situation. Since he couldn't hear the tape either, all he had to go by was the sound meter on the screen. When the level was highest, that meant the laughter was loudest, so Max dubbed those parts opposite his funniest lines. Then he gave himself smaller laughs for the minor jokes.

Mario appeared in the doorway, his coat on. "Sorry, Max, I can't wait any longer."

"I'm done, I'm done!" Max promised. "I just have to burn it on a DVD!" A few seconds later, he pulled the VHS cassette from his entry packet, replaced it with the disk, and resealed the padded envelope. "Go! Go! Go!"

Loyal Mario sprinted for his truck, barely pausing for a quick kiss each from his wife and daughter.

Chapter 8

"Smoke signals. Those were the good old days. No telemarketers. . . ."

"**Y**ou mean you didn't even watch it before you sent it off?" Sydni asked in amazement. She was famous for triple-checking everything.

"There was no time," Max insisted. "The Eggplant Express was ready to roll! As it was, Mario had to fly to meet the FedEx guy outside Piqua. Mom's deducting his speeding tickets from my college fund."

Maude was dubious. "I hope you didn't mess it up. You know—a comedy routine where the laughs come *before* the jokes. They'll think you're an idiot."

"I was careful, okay?" Max assured her. "Everything is going to be fine."

But deep down, he was haunted by doubts.

A week went by, then two, with no word from Chicago. Sydni and Maude stopped mentioning the contest altogether, seeing the reaction of stone-faced misery the subject drew from Max. Big took to blowing mournful renditions of "Taps" through his sinus tubes.

Mario, for one, was unconcerned. "Of course you'll get picked. Who's funnier than you?"

Max appreciated the vote of confidence, but it didn't make him feel much better. Mario laughed when Max read the ingredients off the back of a cereal box. You couldn't go by him.

Come on. Max tried to will his mental messages across the miles to contest headquarters. *Call! Write! E-mail! Fax! Send smoke signals! Just tell me I made it!*

Then came that fateful Friday. Max was in his father's office, waiting to complete the switch to Dad's custody. Noreen, the secretary, was sorting through the mail, when she suddenly announced, "Well, look at this, we got a letter."

When Noreen said *we*, she could have meant

herself, the doctor, a pair of guinea pigs, or five Labrador retrievers who had come in for their shots. It was the only pronoun she ever used. In this case *we* meant Max, who took the envelope she was holding out.

Mr. Maxx Comedy

The hair on the back of his neck stood at attention. The postmark was from Chicago! He checked the return address: The Funniest Kid in America Contest. This was it! In a few seconds he would know if he was in or out.

Hands shaking, he opened the letter:

```
Dear Maxx,
We are sorry to have to inform
you that your audition was NOT
FUNNY ENOUGH to qualify for this
year's contest. We thank you for
your entry, and wish you the
best of luck choosing some other
career.
                    Regretfully,
                    The Judges
```

Max felt his eyes welling up with tears. He hadn't made the cut. And for the worst possible reason! To Max Carmody, no three words were quite so cruel as *not funny enough.*

He was about to rip the letter into a million pieces when he noticed a tiny postscript on the bottom of the page:

P.S.: Just kidding! You're in! Congratulations! Your entry number is 29. The contest is from 2:00–5:00 P.M., so please be at the Balsam Auditorium by 1:30 at the latest. Sorry for pulling your leg, but if you're going to make it in this business, you'd better have a sense of humor.

"I'm in," he barely whispered. Then, a little louder, "I'm in."

"In what, dear?" asked Noreen.

"I'm in!" he howled, enfolding the secretary in a bear hug.

"Mind our makeup, dear," she clucked, dusting herself off.

But Max was too deliriously happy to care. His trick with the laugh track must have worked. He was going to Chicago!

He hugged Mrs. Kaperzinski, parrot cage and all. Then he shook hands with two albino basset hounds, and high-fived a small domesticated pig.

"Oh, this rheumatism!" was Tweedle's comment.

Chapter 9

"Underage. I hate that word. It's like you're still in utero, or something."

With his date with destiny set for November 16, Max's next job was to develop his routine to perfection. Up-and-coming comedians accomplished this by performing every night at local comedy clubs. Of course, most comics lived in big cities like New York and L.A., where there were dozens of places to perform. In Bartonville, Ohio, there was only one: the Giggle Factory on route thirteen, just east of town.

Mr. Lugnitz, owner and manager of the Giggle Factory, reminded Max of one of the Seven Dwarfs. He was a fully grown adult—even a little on the tall side. But his massive head and hulking hands and feet made him look like an enlarged version of a much smaller man. And his personality was a dead ringer for Grumpy.

He listened with a grimace as Max explained that he wanted to be a regular performer at the club in order to hone his act for the contest. "You don't have to pay me anything," Max finished. "And if I win, I promise to mention the Giggle Factory when I go on *Comedy Planet*. That'll be great publicity."

Mr. Lugnitz pointed to a handwritten cardboard sign on the door: UNDER 21 NOT ADMITTED. "You twenty-one?"

"I'm not a customer," Max said seriously. "I'm talent."

"You're underage," the owner corrected. "Why don't you work on your act in front of your little friends at school?"

"I tried that," Max admitted. "But people are really busy over at the middle school. The only class that would let me perform was in-school suspension, and—it's a long story. You don't want to hear it."

Mr. Lugnitz seemed to soften a little. "You go to the middle school? I graduated from there, back when it was the old Bartonville High. Maybe you know my brother's kid, Ronny. I think he's in eighth grade. Real sweetheart."

"Oh, sure, I know Ronny," Max said slyly. In fact, he had never heard of Ronny Lugnitz, and didn't know many eighth graders at all. "We're practically best friends. If he was here, he'd tell you how funny I am. So how about giving me a break?"

"Not a chance, kid."

"Too bad we can't tell him there's a President's Council on Letting Kids Do Comedy," sighed Sydni. She was walking to school with Max, Maude, and Big on Monday morning. "Adults never fall for that one."

"I'm not giving up," Max said determinedly.

"But if the guy doesn't want kids in the Giggle Factory, what can you do about it?"

Max dismissed this with a wave of his hand. "He's just saying that because he assumes I stink. He'd let a three-month-old baby perform if the kid could get laughs. I just have to convince him I'm funny."

"If he won't let you perform, how are you going to do that?" asked Big.

"His nephew goes to our school," Max reasoned.

"All I have to do is find this kid and tell him a few jokes. When he sees how funny I am, I'll get him to put in a word with his uncle."

"Who's the nephew?" asked Sydni.

"He's in eighth grade. Ronny Lugnitz."

Maude blanched. "Ronny Lugnitz? *The* Ronny Lugnitz?"

"Don't tell me he insulted your pants too," Sydni said icily.

"When I went to summer camp," said Maude feelingly, "Ronny Lugnitz snuck over from the boys' compound and put a frog in my sleeping bag every night! By the end of the month, the swamp was practically empty! They had scientists from the university testing the water, trying to find out what happened to the amphibian population!"

"That was two years ago!" Max exclaimed. "He probably doesn't even remember you."

"Oh, yeah? So how come every time I pass him in the hall, he says, 'Ribbit'?"

"Maybe he's not saying 'ribbit,'" mused Big. "Maybe he's saying 'rabbit,' because you have such long ears."

"The guy's evil," Maude insisted. "Half the time he isn't even in the school. He usually skulks around at that big rock just past the fence, where all the juvenile delinquents hang out."

Max nodded. "Then I know exactly where to find him."

"Count me out," said Maude. "I don't go where I'm not wanted."

"In that case," commented Sydni, "you should have spent that eighty-five bucks on a space suit!"

"I'm not going either," put in Big. "I had an artistic inspiration at breakfast this morning. My Alpha-Bits spelled out *tree*. Well, actually, just *tre*, but they never put enough vowels in that cereal. I got the idea to take my video camera and film the first apple falling off Old Atticus."

Old Atticus was the most famous tree in Mercer County. According to legend, it had been planted by Johnny Appleseed himself during his wanderings through Ohio in 1802. The tree overlooked Stryker Pond, which was a gathering point for a flock of Canada geese on their way south for the winter. It was said that, when the first apple fell each October, the geese would leave Bartonville and continue their migration. No one could verify this, of course. No one had ever gone out there to wait for the apple to fall. Until today.

"What? *Now?*" asked Sydni in disbelief. "What about school?"

"That apple won't wait until after three-thirty," said Big firmly. "*Tre* was a sign. It's going to happen today. And it's my job as a filmmaker"—he fluffed up his ascot—"to prove the legend by capturing the moment on video."

"Suit yourself," Sydni groaned. "But if Miss Munsinger asks where you are, I'm not going to lie."

She got no answer. At this point, Big had already split off down the country lane that led to Stryker Pond and Old Atticus.

Nor did Max enter the schoolyard. When Sydni and Maude stepped onto the playground, he skirted the fence and circled around to the big rock that was a magnet for middle school troublemakers and class-cutters.

He found five people there, three boys and two girls. "Hi," he said.

Nobody answered.

"I'm looking for Ronny. Ronny Lugnitz."

"Yo," came a reply.

The boy who stepped forward was compact in every way, slight, skinny, with short limbs, tightly wrapped in denim, top and bottom. Yet he somehow appeared strong, like a coiled spring that could let go at any moment. He took a sip from a can of AMP cola, a drink that was banned at Bartonville Middle School because it had twice the caffeine, four times the sugar, and eight times as much fizz as regular Coke and Pepsi. Mario sometimes drank it. It was popular among truck drivers, because it kept them awake and alert during long hauls.

"Do I know you, kid?"

"Not yet," replied Max smoothly. "I'm Max Carmody, a business associate of your uncle over at the Giggle Factory."

Ronny snorted a laugh that ruffled Max's hair and splashed him lightly with AMP. "Yeah, right."

A tall willowy blond girl with big hair and enough makeup to repaint the school ran up and threw her arms around Ronny. To Max she said,

"Who are *you*?"

"Max Carmody. I'm a comedian."

"Yeah?" She seemed mildly impressed. "I'm Lorelei, Ronny's girlfriend. I like jokes. Tell us a joke."

"One joke wouldn't be enough for a comedy expert like you," Max wheedled. "I know—let me do my whole act for you guys. You can decide if it's funny enough. And," he added with a meaningful look at Ronny, "maybe you'll mention me to your uncle."

"I'm not your agent," Ronny replied. "But I could be your worst nightmare if you don't get lost."

"Do what he says," advised Lorelei proudly. "He can get nasty."

Chapter 10

"If Johnny Appleseed was alive today, he'd be planting arugula."

"It went surprisingly well," Max reported to Sydni and Maude in homeroom.

"Did you ask him to stop saying 'ribbit' every time he sees me?" asked Maude.

"Believe it or not, this wasn't about you. But I met his girlfriend, and we hung out for a while."

"And he's going to talk to his uncle?" prompted Sydni.

"Well, not exactly," Max admitted. "But I got a look inside his book bag, and I saw a work sheet from his language arts class. Mr. Krakauer's doing a unit on humor. I just finished talking to him. He's going to let me perform in front of the class for their end-of-the-unit party. So Ronny will hear my act that way."

Maude rolled her eyes. "All the time I've spent in school, I've never once had an end-of-the-unit party. Is Mr. Krakauer the teacher or the cruise director?"

"It's not exactly the Einstein class," Max explained. "Ronny's in it. If you give them a test, they'll send it back as a paper airplane."

"Big joke," Maude retorted. "You try to entertain that crowd and they'll send *you* back as a paper airplane."

Miss Munsinger breezed in. "I hope everyone had a good weekend." Her eyes scanned the class. "Oh, where's Andrew?"

Sydni, Max, and Maude exchanged an agonized glance. How could they ever explain that their friend Big was sitting in a field, videotaping a tree, waiting for an apple to fall so a bunch of geese could go to Florida?

"Sick," they chorused.

After all, how much of a lie was it?

It was 3:45 by the time Max, Sydni, and Maude arrived at Stryker Pond. There they found Big, his ascot tied around his head to keep his ears warm, fast asleep in the tall grass, the video camera clutched to his chest.

Max reached out and shook Big by the shoulder. "Hey, Steven Spielberg, rise and shine."

Big came awake in a tangle of long arms and legs. "What happened? What happened? Did I miss it?" He looked at the pond, which was still teeming with geese. Except for a few fallen leaves, the ground beneath the old apple tree was bare.

Instead of relief, Big's reaction was impatience. "Hurry up!" he ranted. "Fall already!"

"Be reasonable," argued Sydni. "Just because your cereal said *tre* doesn't mean it's going to happen today. You could be out here all week."

That thought galvanized Big into action. He picked up a rock and heaved it at the tree. It whizzed harmlessly through the branches.

"Hey," mused Maude, "I don't think it counts unless the apple falls naturally."

This seemed to drive Big over the edge. He grabbed an even larger rock, ran directly under the tree, and let fly.

Crack!

An ancient limb broke away and plummeted

straight down. It struck Big across the back of his shoulders, sending him toppling into Stryker Pond with a mammoth belly-flop splash.

The flapping of wings was deafening; the air moved. Hundreds of Canada geese rose from the water as a single unit, falling into their famous V formation as they headed for Fort Lauderdale. In a few minutes, there was nothing but a feather or two to show that they had ever been there.

Teeth chattering, Big heaved himself out of the icy water, his dripping video camera still clutched in his left hand.

Max shook his head. "When it comes to making legends, Johnny Appleseed could have taken lessons from Big!"

The three were ushering their shivering friend back along the dirt road when the NEWS-4 Bartonville mobile van roared up beside them in a cloud of dust. A full TV crew jumped out and immediately covered Big with blankets.

Katie Kates, local reporter, looked daggers at the drenched and shaking boy. "For two weeks we've had a camera trained on that tree, and another one on the pond! No one had ever proven the legend before! What do you have to say for yourself?"

"G-g-great minds think alike?" offered Big.

"You ruined everything!" the reporter stormed. "The geese are gone, the apples are still up there, and the legend goes unproven for another year! I could have had videotape of two centuries of history come to life! Instead, I've got *you*, falling in the pond, giving the geese a heart attack! Nice going!"

"Calm down, Katie," said a cameraman. "The kid's suffered enough. Let's get him home to some dry clothes."

Max spoke up. "Excuse me, Miss Kates. Since you didn't get your local-interest angle, here's something you could report on instead. Did you know that a sixth grader from Bartonville is a finalist in the Funniest Kid in America contest?"

Katie Kates looked right through him, and checked her watch. "It's four-fifteen. If we hurry, we can still catch the lost-puppy story in Blount County."

The film crew drove off with Big. Max, Sydni, and Maude continued up the lane.

Maude was confused. "Hey, Max, why do you want Katie Kates to do a story on you?"

"Don't you get it?" asked Max. "If I go on TV, I

can tell everybody I'm appearing at the Giggle Factory. Mr. Lugnitz will let me go on for sure if I'm bringing him free publicity."

"Well, forget it," said Sydni. "She's never going to report on you. You're not a lost puppy, or a two-hundred-year-old tree, or a Rollerblading great-grandmother."

Max did not reply. An idea was taking shape in his mind.

Chapter 11

"Cat people, make up your minds! Are you cats, or are you people?"

When Max arrived with the cat the next morning, he got exactly the reaction he was hoping for in homeroom 604. His classmates gathered around the pet carrier and reached in to stroke the jet-black fur.

"Is this your cat, Max?" asked Paige McGillis.

"He's nobody's cat," said Max dramatically. "He was abandoned by a family in Chesterland when they moved away. The police picked him up and brought him to my Dad's office."

"That's so *sad*!" exclaimed Brandon Shapiro. "What's going to happen to him?"

Max shrugged soberly. "I was hoping we could kind of take him in as our class mascot—you know, until someone comes along to adopt him."

Miss Munsinger breezed into the room in time to hear the last part. She peered into the cage. "Ooh, he's pretty! Coal-black fur." In her teacher voice, she added, "But it's just not practical. You'll have to take him back where he came from."

"But he's so cute!" Paige protested.

"I agree," said the teacher. "I'm even a cat person. But this is a classroom, not an animal shelter."

"It's just that he was brought to my dad as a stray," Max explained. "If he doesn't get adopted, my father's required by law to put him down."

At that perfect instant, the animal let out a mournful "Mee-ow!" Ten seconds later, homeroom 604 had itself a cat.

Maude leaned over to Max. "All right, Carmody, out with it. I know you're working some kind of angle."

"Of course I am," Max whispered back. "Katie Kates won't do a story on a sixth-grade comedian, but she's going to break her neck getting over here to interview the class that rescued a condemned cat. And if I just so happen to mention on TV that I'm appearing at the Giggle Factory, so much the better, right?"

"Max Carmody, you're disgusting!" snorted Sydni. "Here I thought you were doing something noble for once in your life, and it turns out it's only because of your dumb old comedy!"

Max shrugged. "I admit I got the idea because I'm trying to catch Mr. Lugnitz's attention. But look at it this way. If I didn't bring that cat in here, he'd be dead in a couple of weeks. Now there's a pretty good chance that someone might see him on NEWS-4 news, and adopt him. So even if I'm the biggest sleaze in town, you've got to admit it's a good deal for the cat."

She was unconvinced. "Maybe so. But I think it's sad that you can only do a good deed when there's something in it for you."

"Well, in that case," Max replied, "I guess we shouldn't let the student council cosponsor this. You'd be perfect as the cat liaison person—that would get you back in school government again. But hey, you wouldn't want to benefit from something disgusting. That wouldn't be noble."

Sydni's eyes gleamed. "Amanda Locke is a cat maniac! Max, you're the best!"

By this time, the carrier was open, and the newcomer was climbing on the bookcase. The entire class, Miss Munsinger included, followed behind like a posse, holding out crackers, jelly beans, and half a tuna fish sandwich, hoping to catch his feline fancy.

"What's his name?" asked Brandon.

"He's a stray," the teacher reminded them. "He doesn't have a name. We have to give him one."

As if on cue, the door burst open, and Big Byrd sprang into the room, late as usual. He took one look at the black cat and exclaimed, "Hey, check out Darth Vader!"

And Darth he became.

Cat liaison Sydni Cox placed a call to Katie Kates at NEWS-4 to let her know that homeroom 604 had rescued a cat. As Max predicted, the local reporter jumped at the chance to tell Darth's story to the world or, at least, the greater Bartonville tri-county area.

"She's coming at two o'clock on Friday," Max told Maude. "It'll be a little tight, because I have to do my act for Mr. Krakauer's end-of-the-unit party at two forty-five. But I'll make it. Things are finally starting to fall into place."

"That cat hates my guts," said Maude glumly. "I had an open tin of salmon, and he walked right past me and went over to chew on Big's Popsicle stick."

It was true that a special relationship was developing between Big and Darth. The cat was very much at home with the kids of class 604, and seemed fond of most of them. But with Big it was different. The animal would perch on the teacher's globe, greeting all the students as they arrived, and maintaining a serene, quiet dignity. But when Big made his grand entrance, Darth would pounce. The two of them would roll around on the floor, play wrestling, while Big uttered deep, full-throated Vader-isms, like, "Bring young Skywalker to me," and "Luke, *I* am your father."

And the cat would answer—which always came out "Meow." But it was clear that he was trying to speak.

Sydni was happy too, because she was working for the student council again. Even Amanda Locke had sort of forgiven her, which meant that Sydni could start forgiving Maude. After all, their group of four would probably be friends for life. It would be pretty silly for senior citizens to be still bickering over broken cookies and leather pants from more than fifty years before.

News of the upcoming TV interview spread like wildfire throughout the halls. Darth became a celebrity at Bartonville Middle School. The student newspaper, *The Advocate*, planned to devote an entire issue to class 604's mission of mercy. If there were a few kids who thought a black cat meant bad luck, they kept their opinions to themselves.

"Like a cat could make me any more jinxed than I already am!" Maude snorted.

At night, while Mario raved over the phone about the Voles' upcoming game against the Fighting Lemurs of Youngstown, Max planned his strategy for the interview.

KATIE KATES: How does it feel to know that your idea might very well have saved poor Darth?

MAX: Even though we professional comedians are hired to be funny, it's important to remember that life has a very serious side. . . .

He frowned. Somehow he had to mention the

Giggle Factory. That's what would really get Mr. Lugnitz in his corner.

"You've got to come with me," Mario was urging. "Last time we played the Lemurs, it was the famous Yawn Bowl—six scoreless overtime periods before the snack bar's hot-chocolate machine exploded, and they had to evacuate the building. I didn't get home till four in the morning!"

"Right—uh, that's nice," stammered Max, barely paying attention. Between the interview in seventh period, and his performance in Ronny's class in eighth, he was pretty sure that word of his routine would get through to the club owner. It *had* to!

Mario laughed wanly. "I'll let you go, Max. I can tell you've got something else on your mind. What is it, a new killer joke for Chicago?"

For a moment, Max felt a strange desire to tell his stepfather the whole business about Darth and Ronny and Katie Kates. After all, if there was one adult who could appreciate a scheme like that, it had to be weird Mario, with his beloved Voles, and his tales of record-setting watermelons and the birthplace of the manure spreader.

But Max couldn't bring himself to do it. Aloud, he just said. "A new joke. Yeah, that's it."

Chapter 12

"The government could never build a weapon more dangerous than a jealous boyfriend. . . ."

In all of Bartonville Middle School, no romantic couple was as devoted as Ronny Lugnitz and Lorelei Weiss. One was never seen in the school halls without the other. And they were usually connected, too. They had a special way of melting into each other— her head on his shoulder, his arm around her waist, free hands clasped, legs conjoined as in the three-legged race. Through some miracle of physics, they could actually walk like this, and go up and down stairs.

"That's why they cut so many classes," was

Maude's comment. "They can't get through the door."

"I know one class they'd better not cut," Max muttered darkly.

It was the lone flaw in Max's reasoning. Given Ronny's spotty attendance record, who was to say that he'd even show up for Mr. Krakauer's end-of-the-unit party?

Even so, Max was taken aback on Friday morning to see Lorelei walking toward her homeroom all alone.

Aghast, he rushed up to her. "Lorelei, Lorelei—where's Ronny?"

It took her a moment to recognize Max. "I know you. You're that comedian kid. Funny thing—we're supposed to have a comedian kid in eighth period—"

"That's *me*!" Max explained. "Hey, listen—where's Ronny?"

"Oh," she said, "he got sick."

"No!" Max exclaimed. "He can't miss the end-of-the-unit party!"

"Well," said Lorelei, "to be perfectly honest, they call it a party, but it's really kinda lame. More like school with a bag of chips."

"Maybe he's not really sick!" Max persisted.

"Maybe it's that AMP cola stuff. My stepfather knows a truck driver who got heart palpitations from it!"

"They're pretty sure it's the flu," said Lorelei. "He's got a fever of a hundred and two."

"That's not so high!" Max whined. But his heart was sinking. To parents, the word *fever* was an air-raid siren. The year before, when Olivia had run 102, and Mom had been unable to reach the pediatrician, Mario had diverted from a trip and run an eighteen-wheeler full of kohlrabi directly to the doctor's home. Fevers were the DEFCON 1 of child rearing. "He might feel better by lunch."

Lorelei shrugged one dainty shoulder. "Ronny doesn't come to school half the time when he's feeling fine." And she teetered away on high heels, leaving Max holding his head.

Max gathered up his three friends for advice.

"I don't have time for this," Sydni said briskly. "There's a special student council meeting. Amanda Locke wants to declare Darth official school mascot for all clubs and sports teams. And they have to vote on it before Katie Kates gets here." She bustled off, looking important.

Neither did Maude have anything to offer. "It was a stupid idea to begin with. Ronny Lugnitz is so mean that, even if you had the whole class rolling on the floor, he'd tell his uncle you stank."

Big had a constructive suggestion. "Why don't you go to his house and convince him he should come to school today. Sometimes you have to *make* things happen."

Maude snorted a laugh. "Like you made something happen with Old Atticus?"

"No, this is a good idea!" exclaimed Max. "All I have to do is think of something so compelling it'll make Ronny want to come to school."

Big blew a fanfare through his sinus tubes. "Now, that's a can-do attitude!"

"Let's go," said Max.

"And let Darth face the TV cameras alone?" cried Big in dismay. "Never!"

"What's wrong with going on TV?" asked Maude.

"It's media exploitation," Big insisted. "Nobody asked poor Darth if he wanted to sacrifice his private life."

"What are you raving about?" Max exploded. "His private life is Cat Chow and licking himself!"

"And all that will be over starting today," Big predicted direly.

"Are you crazy?" howled Max. "This is Katie Kates and her little film crew, not *60 Minutes*!"

But Big would not be moved. "Maybe I can't stop it, but I'm not going to let him go through it alone."

Max was nervous. Big didn't get riled up very often. But when he did, he was like a rock and a hard place all rolled up into one. "All right," he sighed. "I'll go with Maude."

"Count me out," said Maude. "All I need is Ronny Lugnitz ribbiting his flu germs in my face! Like I don't have enough problems."

In the end, it was Max alone who snuck out of school just before the lunch bell. In a phone booth, he looked up Ronny's address, and headed to a small, well-kept Cape Cod–style house in the neighborhood just west of the school.

Still not sure what he was going to say, Max rang the front doorbell. He felt a certain confidence that, when the moment came, he would come up with the right thing to tell Ronny. After all, comedians had to be able to think on their feet. What if a heckler showed up in the audience? Max couldn't think of anyone who would make a better heckler than Ronny.

No one answered the door, so he rang again.

"Whaddaya want?" called a voice from above.

Max stepped back and looked. There was Ronny at the upstairs dormer window, staring down, scowling.

"Oh, it's you. What are you doing on my property?"

"I heard you weren't feeling well—" Max began.

"I'm sick as a dog!" Ronny growled. "Leave me alone!"

"Well, it's just that—" Max ransacked his mind for inspiration. He found none. "I'd—uh—hate to see you miss Mr. Krakauer's end-of-the-unit party—"

At this, Ronny stepped away from the window. When he reappeared, it was to dump the entire tank of his cold steam vaporizer down on Max's head.

"Now, scram!"

And it was that icy blast on a cold autumn day that brought Max the brainstorm he needed. "I came here as a friend," he sputtered, "to let you know that some guy is hitting on Lorelei."

Fifteen seconds later, Ronny came out the front door, shivering with fever as he shrugged into his jean jacket. "What guy?" he asked tersely.

"I don't know his name," Max evaded. "He might be new to the school."

"Describe him."

At that moment, Max went completely blank, like no comedian ever should.

Ronny was impatient. "Well, did you see the guy or not?"

"Sure!" Max babbled. He was never really certain why he did it, or even how it came about. But before he knew it, he was describing ". . . a six-foot-tall skinny kid with wild yellow hair, who always wears a red ascot tie."

"I think I've seen this guy," said Ronny grimly. "He was trying to videotape wind. Real artsy type. Does his nose whistle?"

"Absolutely not," said Max, horrified at what he had done. "In fact, he may not have been that tall. And I'm pretty sure his hair was brown."

"Say no more," Ronny insisted. "I know who it is." He popped the tab on a can of AMP. "Man, I feel lousy! Want a sip?"

"Uh—no, thanks." Mission accomplished, thought Max. Ronny Lugnitz was coming to school. He even seemed to be grateful to Max for tipping him off. Now all Max had to do was warn Big. . . .

Max's first class with Big Byrd was science lab in fifth period. To his surprise, Big never showed up, not even ten fashionable minutes late. Odd. Wasn't it Big who'd pledged to be there for Darth for every second of the media blitz that was to come? Where was he?

Probably still in homeroom, Max concluded with an inner smile, holding Darth's paw and whispering warnings: *Luke, Katie Kates has gone over to the Dark Side. But the Force will be with you. . . .*

Either that or Ronny had tracked him down, and the poor kid was in the nurse's office, having his head reattached.

At the next class change, Max found Ronny prowling the sixth-grade hall.

"Pssst! Carmody—over here!" the eighth grader hissed. As the day progressed, Ronny's fever had risen. Now his teeth chattered between guzzles of AMP. "Have you seen you-know-who?"

"No," Max said quickly, "and I'm starting to think it was all a misunderstand—"

"Me neither," Ronny cut him off. "I talked to Lorelei," he confided, bleary-eyed. "She's covering up for the guy. She denies it ever happened."

"Don't be too hard on Lorelei," Max advised guiltily. "It's not her fault if some guy hits on her."

"I'm not holding anything against Lorelei," Ronny replied. "It's that artsy hunk of dogmeat who has to worry."

Max headed straight from Ronny to homeroom 604, but Sydni grabbed him on the way. Her face was even paler than Ronny's.

"Max—he's *gone*!"

"Big?"

"No, Darth! He's disappeared!"

It all came together with a sickening crunch. Big missing + Darth missing = Big and Darth missing together.

"Oh, no!" groaned Max. "Big kidnapped the cat!"

Sydni was aghast. "Why? What for?"

"He thinks the interview is media exploitation! Don't ask why! This is *Big*! The guy videotapes *wind*!"

"But Katie Kates will be here in forty minutes!" squeaked Sydni. "What am I going to do? If I mess up one more thing for the student council, Amanda Locke will have me burned at the stake!"

Her desperation was contagious. Max could see all his careful planning falling apart before his very eyes.

"Don't panic," he said, as much to himself as to her.

"Can you give me one good reason why not?" she shrilled.

"Sydni," called a voice.

Sydni very nearly jumped out of her skin. Amanda was heading down the hall toward her.

"Sydni, we need you to stand at the door and greet the film crew. When they arrive, take them straight to the principal's office. Dr. Mirvish herself wants to introduce Katie Kates to Darth."

As she started away, Sydni cast Max an imploring look, and mouthed the words: *Do something!*

It was like being in the middle of a movie, thought Max. A bad movie, where everything that can go wrong does, and in the worst possible way.

And then it hit him. What did they do on a film set when the star wasn't available?

Answer: a body double.

Chapter 13

"A school library is actually the perfect spot for a life-and-death struggle. . . ."

"This place gives me the creeps," whispered Maude as she and Max let themselves into the waiting room of Dr. Carmody's veterinary clinic.

"Just think of it as a doctor's office," Max soothed. "Only here the patients are animals."

"Animals don't like me," Maude complained. "Look at that ferret over there. See the loathing in his eyes?"

"There's no loathing. It's not a ferret; it's a Beanie Baby. Now, pay attention. We've got a job to do, remember?"

Noreen started when she saw them. "Max!" She

looked at her watch, which told her that the boss's son was here during school hours. "We're not in trouble, are we?" She reached for the intercom.

"No—please," Max begged. "I don't want Dad to know I'm here. Listen—I need another black cat."

"This isn't a lending library, dear," the secretary pointed out. "We can't just come waltzing in here every time—"

"It's just for a couple of hours!" Max pleaded. "It's an emergency! We'll have him back before closing time!"

"Sorry, Max. We have no cats at all."

The intercom buzzed, and Max heard his father's voice. "Noreen, would you come in here, please. It's time to give Percy his shots."

"Coming, doctor." Noreen stood up. "We'd better get back to school," she warned, wagging a finger at Max. And she disappeared into the examining room.

Max checked his watch: 1:40. Katie Kates would be at school in twenty minutes.

"Will you look at this!" Maude exclaimed, nosing around behind Noreen's desk. "People lie right to your face! What kind of a world *is* this?" She bent over and picked up a pet carrier. "She said no cats. What's this—a pterodactyl?"

Max stared. There in the cage, fast asleep, was a black cat. "He's perfect!" he breathed.

"Let's go!" whispered Maude.

"No, wait." Max picked up a pen and scribbled a quick note on Noreen's Post-it pad: "Borrowed cat. Back soon—M."

The two hustled the carrier out the door and down the street.

It was 1:55 by the time they made it back to school. Sydni was at the door to greet them.

"You found him!" she cried in relief.

"Of course," said Maude. "Kind of. Well—not really."

"It's a backup cat," puffed Max, out of breath. "Katie Kates has never met the real Darth anyway."

"The TV people are already here," Sydni said nervously. "They took their equipment up to the library."

The three carried the new Darth upstairs. In the library, the NEWS-4 crew was setting up cameras and lights around Mrs. Gabriel's "Book Nook," which featured dozens of extralarge stuffed animals. Katie Kates herself sat in the librarian's rocking chair, going over her interview notes.

All the students from homeroom 604 gathered

around Max when they saw he had the carrier.

"Where *were* you guys?" demanded Paige.

Max shook his head. "Darth got out of the building somehow. We just managed to coax him back. He's pretty shaken up, so he may not seem like himself for a while."

Everyone watched as Max opened the carrier. The cat stirred, but made no move to leave the cage.

Maude stepped forward. "Come on, Darth," she cooed. "Rise and shine." She reached in and ruffled the black fur. There was an angry meow that was more like a snarl, and a paw that seemed slightly larger than the old Darth's appeared and took a swipe at her arm.

"Yeow!"

The soundman shot them a cockeyed look. "I thought you said he was friendly."

"He's just nervous," put in Sydni. "It must be the hot lights."

Katie Kates stood up. "I'm going to interview several of the kids, and we'll shoot some footage of Darth. Then we'll edit it together into six minutes for the news. Okay, let's start with the vet's son."

Max stepped forward. "Right here."

The reporter looked puzzled. "Don't I know you from somewhere?"

"I don't think so," Max said quickly.

The producer showed Max where to stand, opposite Katie Kates, and right next to an enormous stuffed zebra that was almost as tall as he was.

Katie spoke into the microphone. "I'm here with Max Carmody, a veterinarian's son who is the first of a long line of heroes in this heartwarming story. Max, how did you become aware of this poor, unloved, abandoned animal?"

"Well, I heard about Darth when I was working on my comedy routine. I'm a comedian, as you may know. . . ."

At that moment, a silver-gray Volvo station wagon screeched to a halt in front of the school. Out leaped Dr. Jack Carmody. As he ran for the entrance, he was pulling on a pair of full-length armored gloves, specially designed for handling dangerous animals.

"My local appearances are at the Giggle Factory," Max went on.

"Let's get back to Darth," Katie Kates said through clenched teeth.

But Max was having trouble concentrating on the interview. He had one eye on the cage, where his homeroom classmates were trying to coax Darth out the small opening with a Cat Yummy.

"Darth is the cat equivalent of a nice guy," Max said distractedly. "He wouldn't hurt a flea—of course, he doesn't have fleas!"

There was a sudden noise that fell somewhere between a meow and a shriek. A black blur exploded out of the carrier, shot across the room, and pounced on the plush zebra beside Max.

"And he's so gentle and—uh—lovable and—we really love him. . . ."

As Max babbled, the animal beside him began to dismantle the big toy in a cloud of stuffing.

He heard Amanda Locke's voice: "That doesn't look like Darth!"

In fact, thought Max, heart sinking, it didn't even look very much like a cat!

"Cut! *Cut!*" exclaimed Katie Kates, backing away. "What's wrong with the cat?"

"Isn't he adorable?" blustered Sydni. "He knows martial arts!"

"Sorry I'm late, everyone!" Big peered in from the hall.

"What have you done with our cat?" raged Sydni. "You didn't have the right to kidnap him just because you think this is media exploitation!"

Big was astonished. "I changed my mind about that! I took him to the groomer so he'd look good on TV. See?"

The real Darth appeared at his feet. The black cat now sported a poodle cut.

Miss Munsinger spoke up. "Well, if that's Darth with Andrew—" She pointed to the dark shape at the center of the blizzard of zebra fluff, "then who's *that*?"

The attack on the zebra ceased abruptly, giving everyone a clear look at the imposter. He was a blue-black oversized kitten with yellow-green eyes, and a mouth at least twice the size of a regular cat.

"Everybody *freeze!*" came a command from behind Big. Dr. Carmody stalked into the room, holding his heavily gloved hands out in front of him in the manner of a sleepwalker.

"Hi, Dr. Carmody," said Maude nervously. "We found your cat."

"That's no cat!" the vet exclaimed. "It's a baby panther from the Tri-County Zoo!"

The words were barely out of his mouth when the animal sprang. Students, teachers, and film crew watched in horror as it sailed through the air, coming down right on top of Darth.

Chapter 14

"There is no such thing as a minor problem on the TV news. . . ."

"This is Katie Kates reporting from the veterinary office of Dr. Jack Carmody. On the other side of this door, this compassionate healer works tirelessly to save Darth the cat, an innocent victim of a schoolyard scheme gone horribly wrong. . . ."

"Give me a break!" groaned Max. "He's fine. Dad said it's only a few stitches."

"I should have sacrificed my own body to save him!" Big lamented, dabbing at moist eyes with his ascot.

"You should have stayed in school where you

belonged!" Sydni raved. "But no! You had to get the cat shaved, leaving these two idiots in charge of finding a substitute!"

"How was I supposed to know he was a wild animal?" Maude lamented. "I thought he just didn't like me. Why should he be different from everybody else?"

Luckily, Darth's surgery was a success. But by then he was no longer homeroom 604's special mascot. The Lockes had adopted him. Amanda had telephoned her mother at work, insisting that the family had to save Darth from "the bunch of sickos and Looney Tunes that hang around my ex-assistant on the student council!"

The zoo came to pick up the baby panther around three, and the WBAR crew left shortly after that.

"When is my interview going to be on the air?" Max asked.

Katie Kates glared at him. "When pigs fly, funny boy!"

The only good thing about this, Max reflected morosely, was that today was Friday. He was making the switch to Mom and Mario's, which meant he had a whole week before he would have to face his father over this debacle.

"In *my* world," commented Maude as she walked with Max down Oak Drive toward Chateau East, "this was a pretty average day."

"*Average?*" cried Max. "It was a nightmare! A team of geniuses couldn't figure out a way to make it worse!"

They rounded the corner, and there was Ronny Lugnitz, drooping against a tree. They could almost feel the heat emanating from him as they drew closer.

"Hey, Carmody—you find the guy?"

"Funny thing about that," said Max. "The tall kid has an airtight alibi, so it couldn't be him. We may never know the true identity of the guy who was hitting on Lorelei."

"He's a slippery one," Ronny agreed. "But he can't hide forever." He groaned. "What a lousy day. On top of it all, this comedian kid who was supposed to do a show for our class in eighth period stood us up."

It was the final blow, and Max had no strength left to ward it off. He'd become so wrapped up in the saga of Darth versus the baby panther that he'd forgotten his performance at Mr. Krakauer's class!

Maude was right. Things were never so bad that they couldn't get a little worse.

"My uncle owns a comedy club," Ronny droned on, "and it drives him nuts when the comics don't show up."

"What if there's a good reason?" Maude interjected. "You know—a panther or something."

Ronny fixed him with glassy eyes. "Who are *you*?"

"Maude Dolinka. You remember me. We went to the same summer camp two years ago."

Ronny looked blank. "Whatever. I'm going home." And he teetered off on unsteady legs.

As Max let himself and Maude into Chateau East, his friend was still ranting.

"Can you believe that guy? Pretending he doesn't know me? He put so many frogs in my sleeping bag that I still hear croaking at night!"

"Nobody's here," Max informed him. "Mom takes Olivia to her swimming lesson on Fridays. Let's see if there's any Gatorade."

Depressed and dispirited, they straggled into the kitchen.

"Ronny Lugnitz has been 'ribbiting' at me since I started middle school! Two months of 'Ribbit! . . . Ribbit!'"

"You know what your problem is?" Max interrupted. "You think everybody has nothing better to do than to sit around dreaming up new and exciting ways to disrespect you! No offense, Maude, but you're just not that important!"

He opened the refrigerator. There were no drinks except milk and a single can of Mario's AMP cola.

"Let's try it," said Max, popping the top. "How bad can it be?"

"Count me out," muttered Maude. "I don't want anything in common with Ronny Lugnitz! How could he not know me? Of course he knows me! What other explanation could there be for all that ribbiting?"

Max raised the can to his lips and took a long pull. No sooner did he taste the sugary-sweet liquid in his mouth than he was aware of a cascade of gas bubbles as eight times the fizz of regular soda hit his stomach. A split second later, they were rising, and the burp tore out of his throat:

"Ribbit!"

Chapter 15

"Group therapy is a great idea. Let's get all the crazy people together in one room and let them loose on each other!"

"Parents never warn you about a cold, the flu, a mild viral infection. It's always pneumonia. But when you do get sick, it ends up being some small-time bug that's going around. And they say, 'I told you so.' Just once I wish I had the guts to tell them: 'No, you didn't. You said I was going to get pneumonia.'"

Olivia looked at him blankly. "What's pneumonia?"

Max groaned. "It's what you're going to catch if you don't stay away from me, squirt."

It was new material, created in his 102-degree

haze as Max recovered from the Ronny Lugnitz flu. He couldn't even ask "Why me?", because he knew full well that nobody deserved this more than he did. He had pulled poor Ronny out of his sickbed, run him ragged all over the school in search of Big Byrd, and then told him it was a misunderstanding. He was grateful that fate had decided to punish him for Ronny instead of the kafuffle with Darth. Influenza wasn't fun, but it was better than being mauled by a wildcat.

Another advantage of being under the weather— Max wasn't around for the aftershocks of Panther Day at Bartonville Middle School. Maude filled him in on the lectures about ". . . putting every single solitary soul in this building at risk." The anger and outrage had come from Dr. Mirvish, the librarian, the assistant principal, and Miss Munsinger. During the meeting with the principal, the superintendent had actually called in from his vacation in the Bahamas to voice his displeasure via speakerphone.

Things were worse for Sydni, who was on the student council's Least Wanted list. Amanda Locke had warned her that, if she came anywhere near official activity, the custodian had orders to turn the hose on her.

"All I ever wanted was to be in school government, and it's *never* going to happen," Sydni lamented. "I can't do anything right."

She was so miserable that even Maude felt a twinge of guilt. "You weren't the one who brought the panther to school," she pointed out. "And it was Big who took Darth to the groomer. If anybody was innocent in all this, it was you."

"Innocent, shminnocent," moaned Sydni. "It happened while I was in charge. Politics isn't about whose fault it is. It's about *results*. The only result I ever get is disaster."

There were no signs of Amanda's anger softening. In fact, the girl was becoming more stubborn and bitter every day. There was trouble in the Locke home. Darth, it turned out, was an escape artist. No matter how carefully he was watched and tended, he would find a way out of the house. Worse, once free, he would hightail it into town in search of Big.

On Monday, he tracked the tall boy down at school. At 3:30, Big brought him to his own house. Mrs. Byrd immediately drove Darth to the Lockes. The cat was back on the Byrd doorstep before Big and his mother returned in the car. Now Big's place was permanently on Darth's radar, and there seemed to be nothing the Lockes could do to discourage it.

"Maybe Darth was the wrong name for him," Max commented over the phone. "We should have called him Houdini."

"Big joke!" groaned Maude, who was providing Max with daily phone updates during his illness. "You're safe at home with a thermometer in your mouth! It's the three of us who have to face the music! We're lepers at this school!"

"I'm hurting too," Max assured him. "The Funniest Kid in America contest is in less than two weeks, and I'm going to finish dead last! Without a comedy club to perform at, I'm going to stink out the Balsam Auditorium! My timing will be off, my material will be untested, and I'll probably die of stage fright before I get to my first punch line!"

"Comedy!" Maude practically spat the word. "Don't you see how fed up we all are of you and your stupid comedy? Everything bad that's happened these last few weeks has been thanks to that contest! We're suffering because of *you*, but you can't think of anyone but yourself."

"Suffering?" repeated Max. "Oh, Alert the media, Maude Dolinka is suffering again. You suffer every time the wind blows. You know how fed up you are with my comedy? Triple that, and that's how fed up *I* am with your suffering!"

"Well, maybe I shouldn't burden you with my company, since I annoy you so much," Maude retorted.

"That suits me fine," snarled Max, slamming down the phone.

The remorse came almost immediately. Sure, Maude was a world-class crab. But in a way, her complaining was what had first brought the four friends together, back in second grade.

Nurse Blaff ran a lunchtime group therapy session for troubled kids. The twelve o'clock head-shrinking, Max had called it—even then he'd had a flair for comedy. He was there because his parents had just separated. Maude was there because—well, because she was Maude.

As the weeks went by, others had joined their group. A girl who was despondent because she had lost the election for second-grade representative by three votes. And a tall blond boy fresh out of tonsil and adenoid surgery. Now that he had discovered the musical tubes in his sinuses, how could he be expected to resist playing them?

"I've got a symphony in my nose," the five-foot-six seven-year-old had greeted the group. "Listen to this!"

The four came together under the banner of Maude and her complaining. There was something about the girl's hard-luck life that made their own problems easier to take. No sob story was ever so awful that Maude couldn't chime in with, "You think that's bad? Wait till you hear what happened to *me*!"

Now Max was about to step out into the bright lights of the Balsam Auditorium completely unprepared. If there was ever a time when he needed his best friend, this was it.

He called a few times, but Maude's line was always busy. Guessing that she was probably surfing the Internet, he booted up the iMac and instant-messaged her:

```
Maude,
Come to Chicago with me. I can't
face the contest without you.
—Max
```

Her reply was onscreen in less than thirty seconds:

```
Okay, but only if I get the front
seat.
```

By the time Max was back in school, a whole week had passed, and the contest was the coming Saturday. He approached Mr. Krakauer for another shot at performing for his English class.

"Forget it, Max. I don't make any more appointments with you."

So much for Max's last chance to impress Ronny and maybe get in at least one set at the Giggle Factory. On Saturday, he would be facing the judges stone cold.

He was surprised when Mario called him at Dr. Carmody's house. Max knew it wasn't just to update him on his stepfather's latest exotic location—Brooklyn, New York, in the shadow of the largest sewage facility in the nation.

"I always thought that was in the back of your truck," Max quipped. He held the phone away from his ear as Mario's booming laughter rattled the receiver. "What's up?"

"Listen, kiddo," his stepfather managed finally, "I've got some crummy news. Three drivers are out this week, and I've got to make the Saturday run myself. There's no way I can get to your contest."

Max began to panic. "But Mom won't want to go to Chicago without you!"

"It stinks, I know," Mario said sadly. "But it's work. What can I do?"

All at once, Max wanted to lash out. The words formed in his mind: *My real father wouldn't blow me off like this!*

But even as he thought it, he knew it was unfair. Dr. Carmody had business responsibilities too. He had dragged four kids to the Plandome farm at nine o'clock at night when Madonna had gone into labor. Besides, who was more supportive of Max's comedy than Mario? It wasn't right to blame this on him.

"You mean—" He could barely bring himself to say the words. "You mean I'm going to have to—drop out?"

"Well—" There was genuine anguish in Mario's voice. "Let me talk to your old man for a minute."

Max waited breathlessly as his two fathers, step and regular, managed to hash out a backup plan. Dad would take Max to Chicago in the Volvo, along with Mom, Olivia, and Maude, whose parents had said yes to the trip. They would leave Saturday morning, attend the contest, stay overnight in a hotel in Chicago, and return on Sunday.

"In other words, you can kiss the front seat good-bye," Max told Maude. "But at least we're still going."

Maude had another concern. "Your mom and dad in the same car for four hours? Have they been together for that long since the divorce?"

"If you want to back out, I won't stop you," Max offered.

"Believe me," said Maude, "if this contest ends up a catastrophe, you'll be grateful for my moral support."

"I'm prepared for a catastrophe," replied Max grimly. "I just hope it doesn't happen in the car before we even get there!"

Chapter 16

"I get carsick on long drives—as in, sick of the car. . . ."

Saturday could not have been more miserable—cold and foggy, pouring buckets of frigid rain. Maude's alarm clock failed to go off, so she had to be hauled bodily out of bed at departure time, eight A.M. She groggily tossed some clothes and toiletries in an overnight bag and crawled into the backseat of the Volvo with Max and Olivia.

Olivia had to stop to go to the bathroom twice before they left the Bartonville city limits. By the second stop, she—and the Volvo's leather seats—were drenched with rain.

It didn't take much longer than that for Max's mother and father to remember why they had gotten divorced in the first place.

"Do you have to drive like that?" Ellen Plunkett complained.

"Like what?" asked Dr. Carmody innocently.

"With your seat reclined halfway to the tailpipe. You look like you're propped up to read in bed."

"The ancient Romans used to eat in the reclining position," he argued.

"Maybe so," said his ex-wife. "But they didn't do it while driving their chariots. Hey, you missed the turn."

"No, I didn't."

She pointed behind them. "The sign said Route forty-four!"

"I know a short cut," he insisted.

Maude watched in horror as Max took out his tape machine and placed the headphones over his ears. "What are you doing?" she hissed.

"I've got a cassette of my act in here," Max explained. "It can't hurt to do a little last-minute cramming."

"But you can't leave me alone"—she dropped her voice to a whisper and motioned toward the front seat, where Max's parents were still bickering—"with *them*!"

Max shrugged. "I gave you the chance to back out." He hit PLAY and retreated into the world of his comedy.

Maude slumped back against the leather, exasperated.

Olivia looked at her earnestly. "My brother's going to be famous after today."

Maude snorted under her breath. "Yeah, sure."

"He's going to be on TV. I wonder if I'll get to be on TV with him."

Maude shot her friend a withering glare and replied, "Why not? You'd be a lot less ugly!"

That was all Olivia had to hear. "You think I'm pretty?"

"Better than him, that's for sure," sneered Maude.

Olivia tried to sidle over on her booster seat toward the older girl. "My daddy says I'm a princess. Do you think I'm a princess?"

"I'm not too big on royalty," Maude replied. "I had an asthma attack at Buckingham Palace last summer."

Olivia regarded her with deep respect. "You went to a real palace?"

Maude nodded. "They had a bunch of princesses there. Princes, too. Even a queen. I never figured out what they did with the king. He can't be very popular, because *her* face got to be on all the money."

Dr. Carmody reached over and nudged his ex-wife's arm. "Are you following that little civics lesson in the backseat? Your daughter could learn a lot from Maude Dolinka."

"Bite your tongue," she groaned. "Six billion people on this planet, and Livy has to pick this one as a role model."

"I think it's cute," Dr. Carmody teased.

"That's because she isn't your daughter," she muttered. "And I'm pretty sure we're lost."

"We're fine. We should hit Indiana in an hour or so."

It was not often that Maude had an audience hanging on her every word. So she launched into a speech on her favorite subject—why the odds were always stacked against her.

"It all started on December nineteenth, 1992, the day I was born. The hospital ran out of pink blankets, so I had to have a blue one. My mother said everybody thought I was a baby boy, as if I had a mustache or something. Even today I feel the cold sting of humiliation from that moment casting a shadow over everything I do."

"Wow," breathed Olivia.

"Day care was tough," she continued bitterly. "It wasn't all purple dinosaurs and finger paint like it is for you kids today. How was I supposed to know fish don't like ice cream? The water got so cloudy they couldn't even see to pluck the bodies out. The teacher deliberately put my diaper on wrong every day."

It went on. Problems in preschool. Calamities in kindergarten. There was a separate tale of woe for every grade at Bartonville Elementary.

Olivia listened, her blue eyes widening until they were like half-dollars. In the front seat, the adults were focusing their attention on the road, which was becoming narrower and bumpier, leading through towns with names that were no longer familiar.

"This can't be right," Mrs. Plunkett said sharply.

"It has to be," replied her ex-husband. "See? Here's the highway."

Alas, the approaching sign did not point the way to the interstate. It read simply PAVEMENT ENDS.

The Volvo bounced along the dirt road, stopping for cows that wandered out of the fog.

Max pulled off the headphones. "Well, I *hope* I'm ready—" He took in his surroundings in dismay. "Is *this* the way to Chicago?"

Chapter 17

" Mothers always want to stop to ask for directions. Fathers never do. . . ."

"**W**e're not lost," Dr. Carmody insisted. "We just— don't know where we are."

Max's mother had had enough. "Oh, yes we do, Jack Carmody. We're nowhere! Now turn right around and we'll ask directions at the next farm- house."

The problem was that, in the rain and mist, it was hard to see anything more than fifty feet away, let alone a farmhouse set well back from the road.

They had been wandering for about an hour when Max started looking at his watch. "It's ten-thirty. We need to be in Chicago in three hours. Can we get there in three hours, Dad?"

"Oh, sure," Dr. Carmody blathered. "No problem."

"I think we've been driving around in circles," Maude observed bleakly.

Max was alarmed. "Why do you say that?"

She pointed. "We've passed that same cow twice before."

"How do you know it's the same one?" asked Dr. Carmody. "All cows look alike."

"She's scowling at me," the girl replied seriously.

"Maude has a hard life," Olivia explained.

Max glared at his best friend. "Have you been brainwashing her?"

"I told her the truth, the whole truth, and nothing but the truth," Maude said, defensively.

Suddenly, Dr. Carmody stomped on the brakes, and the Volvo lurched to a stop in a shower of slime and dirty water. Only their seat belts kept the passengers from sailing through the front windshield.

"Jack, are you crazy?" railed Mrs. Plunkett. "You're going to get us all killed!"

Max's father burst out of the car and ran up to an ancient dirt-covered sign. He popped the trunk and went to work on the crusted mud with the ice scraper. After a few minutes of chipping and scrubbing, the long-lost message began to appear through the muck:

ROUTE 44—19 MILES ⟶

"The highway!" cried Max.

Filthy and sopping wet, his father jumped back behind the wheel and threw the car in gear. "Hang in there, kid! I told you we'd make it!"

As they jounced along the dirt road, the Volvo became the scene of the kind of mathematical calculations that normally took place only in physics labs. It was eleven o'clock. The Balsam auditorium was 240 miles away.

"Which means," Max concluded excitedly, "if we go eighty, we'll make it just in time for the two o'clock start!"

"You can't go eighty on a dirt road," Dr. Carmody called back from the driver's seat.

"You can't go eighty on *any* road," amended his ex-wife sternly.

"We can slow to fifty on the unpaved portion," Maude agreed, expertly crunching numbers in her head, "if we bump it up to eighty-five once we hit the Interstate." At that moment, the Volvo's tires jumped from the rutted mud and stones onto a bumpy but paved two-lane farm route. "This is better. How fast can we go here?"

"At least seventy," put in Max.

"No!" stormed Ellen Plunkett. "We'll drive the speed limit and get there late, but in one piece."

"Come on, Ellen," coaxed Dr. Carmody. "This is a big day for Max. We've got a chance to make it!"

No sooner had the words crossed his lips than steam began billowing up from under the Volvo's hood. Dr. Carmody pulled over to the shoulder and rushed around to the front of the car. The hot blast burned his hands as he threw open the hood. *"Yeow!"*

"Jack, are you all right?" cried Max's mother in alarm.

"I'm fine, but the radiator isn't," her ex-husband moaned.

"It's fixable, right?" Max called out the window. "Can you fix it?"

His father drew a deep breath. "A mechanic can—in about three hours."

"No-o-o-o-o!!"

"Oh, boy." Mrs. Plunkett looked around. They were absolutely in the middle of nowhere. The only break in the trees and scrub—the only indication that the area was even inhabited—was a single faded sign:

COLDWATER 5

VAN WERT 41

CHICAGO 238

Olivia looked at Maude in awe. "You're right! Bad things really *do* happen to you!"

"To *her*?" Max was practically hysterical. "To *her*? What about to *me*? Comedy is my whole life! I'm nothing without it! And finally, even though I live in a town where everybody thinks I stink and my dreams are stupid, I get a chance to prove myself! And where am I when my date with destiny rolls around? Freezing in the rain in a ditch outside Coldwater, Ohio!"

His parents exchanged an unhappy glance. Ellen Plunkett and Jack Carmody didn't agree on much. But it pained them to see their son so crestfallen. Even Maude had no comment. Then:

"Coldwater, Ohio?" Olivia repeated. "Isn't that the town where the manure spreader was invented?"

Chapter 18

"Who picked eighteen as the number of wheels for a tractor-trailer?"

"That's right!" Max grasped at the information like a drowning man clinging to a life preserver. "Mario passes here all the time! Wasn't he supposed to come through today?"

There was a frantic cell phone conversation, and Mrs. Plunkett delivered the news. "He'll be here in forty-five minutes."

Max jumped up and down like a madman, pumping his fist in the air. "Yes! Yes! Yes! Way to go, Mario! You're my man!" To his father, he added, embarrassed, "And you too, Dad. Thanks for—uh—getting us this far."

Dr. Carmody ruffled his son's unruly hair. "I hope you make it, Max."

It was going to be close. They would be late—there was no question about that. And a big rig like Mario's wouldn't be able to drive as fast as Dr. Carmody's Volvo. But if they could just get to the Balsam Auditorium before the contest ended at five o'clock, Max could explain what had happened, and maybe the judges would let him go on last. It was a slim chance, but the only one he had.

It was after one when Mario's eighteen-wheeler roared up the two-lane farm road to the incapacitated Volvo. Dr. Carmody had to stay to wait for the tow truck. Mrs. Plunkett, Max, Maude, and Olivia wished him good-bye and good luck.

There wasn't enough room in the cab for all five of them, so it was decided that Mrs. Plunkett and Olivia would ride up front with Mario. Max and Maude were relegated to the cheap seats in the refrigerated trailer with the cargo.

Mario led them around the back and opened the big cargo door. The container was piled high with boxes.

"There's no room," Max protested.

"Just wedge yourself between the cartons and hold on tight," Mario advised cheerfully. He tossed his stepson a flashlight. "It's dark with the door closed."

"It's freezing back here," Maude complained. "By the time we get to Chicago, we'll be in suspended animation!"

"There's no extra charge for the air-conditioning," grinned Mario. And he slammed the door and latched it, leaving them in the chilly blackness. A moment later, they heard the roar of the motor, and the truck began to move.

Max switched on the flashlight and played the beam over the piled cartons. "I wonder what this stuff is. It just says 'perishable' on the side."

"I hope that doesn't mean us," sniffed Maude. "I feel like I'm going to perish any minute."

They found a stack of tarpaulins and each took one to use as a blanket against the chill air. "Mario drives me nuts," Max confessed. "But I don't think I've ever been so happy to see anybody!" He closed his eyes and concentrated on the motion of the trailer, trying to estimate their speed. Could the eighteen-wheeler go fast enough? It would be a tragedy beyond words to go through all this and *still* miss the contest.

Max wasn't a very patient car passenger in the best of circumstances. His nervousness and the cold and discomfort of the truck combined to make the time creep along agonizingly slowly. His act played itself out again and again in his head, the jokes rattling painfully around his brain. And it didn't help to have to listen to the rustling and shuffling of Maude fidgeting under her tarpaulin.

"Quit it," Max complained. "I'm uncomfortable too, okay? This isn't exactly my idea of first-class travel."

Her jerky movements only grew more exaggerated. "That's not it. I'm itchy!"

"It's all in your head," Max explained patiently.

"No! I itch all over!"

"Cut it *out*—" But when Max shone his flashlight beam at his best friend, he saw that her face was covered in bright red blotches. "Maude—you're breaking out!"

"Oh no," she cried, "I'm allergic to the truck!"

"No one can be allergic to a truck," argued Max. "Not even you."

"But—" Maude leaped to her feet. "What's in these boxes?"

She ripped the nearest one open. It was packed with—

"Cherries!!"

Chapter 19

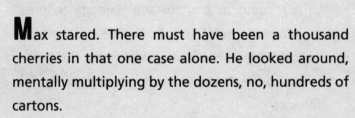

"Whoever said 'Life is a bowl of cherries' is the pits."

Max stared. There must have been a thousand cherries in that one case alone. He looked around, mentally multiplying by the dozens, no, hundreds of cartons.

"I'm allergic to cherries! I've got to get out of here!" Crawling over the cargo, Maude made her frantic way to the back and yanked on the latch to the cargo door.

Max grabbed her from behind and wrestled her away. "Are you crazy? What are you going to do, jump out of a speeding truck into four lanes of oncoming traffic?"

"But there's enough cherries in here to kill me fifty times!" She pushed her way to the front of the container and began pounding against the wall. "Stop the truck!"

Out of options, Max joined her. "Mario!" he yelled. "Mom! We've got a problem!"

"They can't hear us!" lamented Maude. She picked a crowbar up off the floor and started banging with that.

"Careful!" Max admonished. "If you dent the trailer, they might make Mario pay for the damage!"

"Who's going to pay for the damage to *me*?" wailed Maude. "Help! Help!" She reared back for one monster blow, but instead delivered the home-run swing to the container's refrigeration unit.

Thwack!

The heavy metal ripped the hose clear off the compressor. Dense white mist hissed out of it, filling up the trailer like a fog.

"You *idiot*!" lamented Max. "Mario's going to kill us!"

Up front in the cab, Olivia was the first to notice the blinking red warning light on the dashboard. "What's that, Daddy?"

"Uh-oh," said Mario. "Refrigeration failure." He pulled over to the shoulder and jumped out, hurrying to the passenger side to help his wife and daughter down from the big rig. The three rushed to the back of the trailer. Mario unhooked the latch and rolled up the cargo door.

A dense cloud of escaped refrigerant billowed out, followed by two coughing sixth graders.

"Maude!" cried Olivia with relief. "You're okay!"

"I'm fine too, thanks," muttered Max, jumping to the road. "Remember me, your brother?"

Mario helped Maude out of the truck.

Mrs. Plunkett stared in alarm at the fire-engine-red rash on Maude's face. "My God, Maude, what happened to you?"

"Cherries!" Maude spat. "Millions of them! I'm lucky to be alive."

Waving his arms to dispel the mist, Mario climbed into the trailer and snaked his way back between the stacks of boxes. "No wonder the cooler's leaking. The hose is detached. Did it just pop clean off like that?"

"Kind of," admitted Max. "When Maude hit it with a crowbar."

"Well, I had to get your attention," Maude

explained to Mario. "I was trying to bang on the wall but I missed."

Mario squinted through the fog at the blotches on Maude's face. "It could happen to anybody," he said dubiously.

"Not anybody," Olivia corrected proudly. "Just Maude."

Her father swallowed hard. "We're just glad you're okay."

"What about the cherries?" Max's mother asked in concern. "With the refrigeration unit on the fritz, won't they go bad?"

Her husband looked thoughtful. "Not necessarily . . ."

It was a quiet moment in the hectic weekend schedule of downtown Chicago. The day-trippers had already left, but the dinner and theater crowd had not yet arrived.

That calm was shattered at precisely two minutes to five o'clock, when a massive tractor-trailer came barreling up State Street at breakneck speed. The cargo door was wide open, exposing eighty-seven large cartons of Bing cherries to the crisp November air.

The eighteen-wheeler squealed to a halt in front

of the Balsam Auditorium, and out of the back leaped Max Carmody. His normally messy hair had been so blown around by the wind that it stood on end as if he had been filled with static electricity.

He hit the ground running. *"I'm he-e-e-ere!"*

Maude jumped out of the cab in hot pursuit, her red allergic rash slightly faded. "I'm right behind you, Max!"

Olivia was next. "Maude—wait for me!"

"Livy—come back!" Mrs. Plunkett tried in vain to rein in her young daughter. She gave her husband a quick kiss. "You were a real hero today, Mario. Sorry about the truck. I hope the cherries don't spoil."

"They'll be fine," he assured her. "I'll take the northern route. There's a cold front dipping down from Canada." He hopped back up to the cab and called, "Break a leg, Max!"

Right before the heavy brass doors of the Balsam Auditorium, Max froze. The time pressure was unbelievable—it was ninety seconds to five. Yet there was something that had to be said.

It was probably too late anyway. But Max wouldn't have made it here, would have had no chance at all, had it not been for his stepfather. The guy had driven hours out of his way, and risked an expensive perishable cargo, just to get Max to Chicago. It was more loyalty than Max could have expected from anybody, and a heck of a lot more than he had the right to expect from Mario—someone he'd never been very nice to.

He turned to face his stepfather, who was just about to pull away from the curb. "Hey, Mario—do the Voles have any home games coming up?"

Mario grinned. "Next Wednesday. A grudge match with Caveman Ogrodnick and the Mansfield Mayhem."

"Save me a ticket!" yelled Max, and blasted through the auditorium doors.

He didn't even hear the "Can I help you, son?" from the man in the glass booth. It was five o'clock on the nose, but these things never finished on time, right? There was still a chance! There had to be!

He plowed blindly through the velvet curtain and pounded down the aisle between the packed rows of seats toward the spotlit stage.

"And now, the moment we've all been waiting for," the emcee was announcing. "The judges have reached their decision. The Funniest Kid in America is—" Kettledrums built to a dramatic crescendo— "Barry Robson!"

All the steam went out of Max, and he coasted to a stop on the red carpet. He was amazed he didn't fall flat on his face.

Barry Robson.

The name ricocheted around his head like an accelerated particle as his stomach tied itself into a knot worthy of an eagle scout.

Barry Robson, The Funniest Kid in America.

Not Maxx Comedy. Not Max Carmody.

He watched through eyes filling up with tears as an ecstatic young teen ran onstage to accept a large trophy featuring a gleaming silver microphone. His disbelief melted into despair. They had gone through so much today—getting lost, the break-down, Maude's allergy attack, Mario's busted cool-ing unit. Yet, against all odds, they had made it to Chicago and the Balsam Auditorium.

But not in time.

The contest was over.

Chapter 20

"A funny thing happened to me in Chicago. . . ."

Their motel was a pleasant little roadside inn on the outskirts of Chicago. But not even the cheery rooms and 140 cable channels could brighten the deep, dark depression that had settled over Max Carmody.

One at a time, his traveling companions tried to lighten his mood.

"I'll watch you do your act any time you want," Olivia offered generously. "You can even make fun of Barney."

"Forget it, kid," her brother muttered. "After today, I'm through with the comedy business. I'm never going to tell another joke as long as I live."

Mrs. Plunkett was next. "Well, the cherries are safe and the truck is fixed," she reported. "Mario just called in from Montague, Iowa. Did you know that's the home of the world's largest fire hydrant?"

"Uh-huh."

His mother regarded him expectantly. "Don't you have anything to add to that, Maxie?"

"If I still made jokes, which I don't," Max replied, "then I might say that I hope the dogs in that town are all ten feet tall. But that would be funny, and there's nothing funny about my life right now."

Last came Maude. She waited until Mrs. Plunkett and Olivia had retired to the girls' room next door. "You think this is bad?" she challenged. "This is *nothing*. Try walking a mile in my shoes, and I don't mean just because of the orthotic insoles for flat feet. *I'm* the world's largest fire hydrant, pal. And there are a lot of dogs out there—of all sizes."

Max looked daggers at her. "It's reassuring to know that, after everything that happened today, this is really all about *you*." He pointed to the door. "Get out of here. I want to be alone."

"What about TV?" Maude switched on the set and deposited herself on one of the beds. "Your mom would never let me watch Chicago news in front of Olivia. The big-city crime is way better than the wimpy stuff that happens at home. In Bartonville, breaking news is Katie Kates sobbing because somebody backed over a caterpillar."

As Maude drank in stories of fires, armed robberies, and high-speed police chases, Max barely heard a word. For two whole months, every fiber of his being had been focused on this contest. Now it was over, and without his firing off so much as a single punch line. It was like losing a war before you could pick up a peashooter in your own defense. And on top of it all, Max now had a date with Mario to see Caveman Ogrodnick and his merry Neanderthals. It was the end. It was more than he could bear.

"Hey, look." Maude pointed at the screen. "They're talking about your contest."

Max picked up the remote and hit MUTE. "I'm not listening."

"There's the guy who won," she went on. "Hey, that's a nice trophy." She reached for the clicker. "Come on, let's listen to the acceptance speech."

"No."

Max tried to yank the remote away, but Maude

grabbed on. There was a brief tug-of-war, and then the sound returned—the winner's standing ovation. For Max it was a hammer blow to the heart.

The applause died away and the anchor returned. "There was one additional award, although for some reason, this young comic never got to perform. The chief judge explains. . . ."

Onscreen, the contest official was being interviewed backstage. "We didn't plan on this, but we got a video that you just can't ignore. The whole committee made copies because it's something you want to keep forever. It's the funniest bit I've ever seen. If you're out there, Maxx Comedy, you've got a great future."

Max froze as his audition video began to play right there on the Chicago news.

There was Max, larger than life, on the stage of the Bartonville Middle School gym, as Big Byrd had filmed him a month earlier. "In our school cafeteria," he began his routine, "the black-bean burrito has been designated a weapon of mass destruction."

Holding his breath, Max waited for his laugh track to kick in. And, yes, there was a huge reaction. But it was not the howls of mirth he had taped at the Locke party. The sound that swelled through the TV's small speaker was horrible, violent, *animal*. . . .

Maude's jaw fell open. "What's *that*?"

How *would* you describe it? A frantic, agonized combination of moaning, howling, and shrieking. Almost—

"*Mooing?*" Max exclaimed in disbelief.

"Yeah!" Maude snapped her fingers in sudden recognition. "I haven't heard anything like that since your dad gave birth to that cow!"

Strictly speaking, Dad had *delivered* the calf. He was the vet, not the mother. But Max never said this out loud. Because at that instant, everything became crystal clear to him in a flash of sudden, amazing, and terrible understanding.

"It *is* that cow!" Max rasped, awestruck. "Somehow, in the Plandome barn that crazy night, I must have turned on my tape machine by mistake and recorded Madonna giving birth over my laugh track!"

Maude was bewildered. "But why didn't you listen to it before dubbing it onto the audition tape?"

"I couldn't!" Max lamented. "My dad lost the tape machine before I woke up the next morning. And by the time I got it back, Mario was leaving, and the computer's speakers were broken, and—I can't believe it!"

They watched as Max went through his entire act, with each joke being greeted by wild mooing. He had timed it perfectly on the computer. Every blast of bovine labor came exactly where the audience response should have been. Given a real laugh track, and not a recording of a livestock blessed event, he would have succeeded one hundred percent.

He cradled his head in trembling hands. "This is bad. This is worse than bad. I'd need a million-percent improvement to get this up to bad!"

"What are you talking about?" asked Maude, listening intently. "You're a smash!"

As the audition tape played, the news anchor, sports reporter, weatherman, and the entire studio crew could be heard howling in the background.

"I'm a joke," Max amended miserably. "The audience is supposed to laugh *with* you, not *at* you."

When it was finally over, the anchor was wiping tears from her eyes as she struggled to regain her composure for the rest of the broadcast. "Maxx Comedy, ladies and gentlemen," she managed. "Remember that name. Coming soon to a barnyard near you."

"See?" moaned Max. "I'm a laughingstock."

"At least it's just in Chicago," Maude offered in consolation. "Nobody knows you around here, anyway."

The phone rang.

Max answered it. "Oh, hi, Dad," he said listlessly. "How's the car?"

Dr. Carmody was in a state of excitement. "I got home an hour ago. But never mind that. Listen, Max, what went on at the contest? I just took a call from a guy named Frank Lugnitz who saw you on TV!"

"Really?" Max was confused. "How does Mr. Lugnitz get Chicago TV all the way in Bartonville?"

"He says he saw you on CNN! According to him, your tape is on all the comedy channels too! What happened? Did you win that contest?"

"Not exactly," Max said shakily. "But I guess people kind of like my audition video."

"Like it?" Max's father was almost shouting now. "The man wouldn't shut up about how great you are! He owns the Giggle Factory, and he wants to hire you to perform! He says you're the funniest kid in America!"

Chapter 21

"And now, the moment you've been waiting for . . . total mayhem!"

Max's professional comedy debut at the Giggle Factory was scheduled for Sunday afternoon at two o'clock. Mr. Lugnitz was so excited to have Max on his roster that he made an exception to the club's "no kids" rule. Max's famous audition tape had made the rounds of every newscast on the continent, and the place was packed. Barry Robson may have been the official Funniest Kid in America, but nobody had ever heard of him. In the tri-county area at least, Maxx Comedy was a household word.

It seemed like half of Bartonville Middle School

was there. Many paid tribute to Max's audition tape by appearing in cow hats, waving pictures of cows, ringing cowbells, and holding up hand-lettered MOO signs. The drink of the day was, of course, milk—chocolate, strawberry, and straight up.

In the front row, in specially reserved seats, were Maude, Sydni, and Big, closest friends of the headliner.

Big Byrd was wearing his ascot again. As the cameraman of the famous audition tape, he had decided that his film career was finally taking off, so he intended to look the part.

Sydni was glancing nonchalantly over her shoulder, trying to see if any of the student council was in attendance. Her star was rising in school government again, thanks to Max. He had pledged some of today's appearance fee to repay the eighty-five dollars from Maude's leather pants. Sure enough, quite a few members were there. But, Sydni noted with a sigh, Amanda Locke was not one of them.

She felt a tap on her arm, and turned to see none other than Kelly Latanzia, the student-council president. Eighth-grade Kelly was the most popular girl in school, not to mention Amanda Locke's *boss*! She had never spoken directly to Sydni before.

Kelly was oozing charm. "We just wanted to thank you for all the great work you've been doing for the student council. Keep it up. We've got our eyes on you."

"Uh—you're welcome," Sydni stammered in amazement. What was going on here? Amanda hated her guts. Yet here was the top dog herself being so nice. "Sorry for all the—you know—all that."

"Ancient history," Kelly assured her, dismissing the past with a wave of her hand. "We're focusing on new stuff now. Like Harvest Festival. I hope you'll help us with the student council's booth." She added meaningfully, "You and Max."

"Of course!" Sydni beamed. "I've got tons of ideas! Big can be our official videographer! And Maude can—"

"Well, it's a pretty small booth," Kelly cut her off. "We don't want to let it get too crowded."

"But Big's a fantastic cameraman," Sydni insisted. "And Maude's a good worker—if you don't put her in charge of any money."

Kelly leaned forward confidentially. "The truth is, Sydni, you're okay, and Max is practically famous. But this is a student-council thing, and we don't want to let too many sixth graders in on it. You know what I mean."

Sydni flushed, staring at the president in sudden understanding. Kelly didn't want *her*. She was just using her to get to Max, who was a celebrity because of the contest. Maude and Big didn't even make the guest list.

"Sorry, Kelly," she said briskly, "I'm pretty sure I'm going to be washing my hair all those days. I just signed up with the President's Council on In-School Civility, and they have a strict no-snob policy."

Kelly's jaw dropped. "We didn't want you any-way!" she seethed, storming away.

Big gave a long whistle of admiration through his left sinus tube. "Whoa, Sydni, that was *huge*! You just blew off the big enchilada!"

"It was awesome," added Maude.

Calm down, Sydni told herself, her pounding heartbeat resounding in her ears. She may have just insulted the entire student council, but there was still Amanda Locke. All Sydni needed was another chance to talk to her. . . .

Backstage, Max was living his dream. This was even better than winning the contest. The sight of his name on the marquee outside the Giggle Factory had put a smile on his face so wide that his cheeks hurt. It was impossible to frown. He actually tried, but he couldn't force the corners of his mouth to turn down. It was almost as if Fate were making up for all the rotten luck that had dogged him these past few weeks.

Whatever the reason, he was about to perform for an adoring crowd. True, they were only fans because of a bizarre and almost terrible mistake. But it had turned out great. Better than great. Perfect.

Mr. Lugnitz was happy too. "It's a packed house out there, Max! How do you feel, kid?"

"Awesome!" exclaimed Max. It was the understatement of the year.

Ronny Lugnitz was there with his uncle. "I gotta hand it to you, Carmody. I always thought you were a total loser." He took a swig of his AMP cola. "But that cow routine—me and Lorelei were laughing our heads off! And to think I dumped out my humidifier on you! How cool is that?"

"Thanks," said Max. A star had to be gracious.

Mr. Lugnitz checked his watch. "Okay. Two o'clock. Showtime."

He stepped out from the wings and instantly

drew a spotlight. "Welcome to the Giggle Factory, the tri-county area's only *family* comedy club. Let's give a warm welcome to Bartonville's own *Maxx Comedy*!"

For the first time, Max took center stage, amid thunderous applause and full-throated mooing from the audience.

He hefted the microphone. "Thank you, thank you—"

And then, from the wings, Ronny Lugnitz spotted Big Byrd sitting in the front row.

"That's him!" came a roar that drowned out even Max's ovation. *"That's the guy who was hitting on Lorelei!"*

So, instead of his carefully crafted opening joke, Max began his comedy career with: "Run, Big! He's going to kill you!"

Ronny sprang across the stage, almost knocking Max over. AMP cola sprayed everywhere.

In a tangle of long arms and legs, Big Byrd scrambled out of his seat a split second before Ronny's fist got there.

"What did I do?" the tall boy howled, his nasal tubes whining in harmony with his words. But although he was pretty sure of his innocence, Big was taking no chances. He made a beeline for the exit, his imitation-silk ascot flapping behind him. Ronny was in hot pursuit.

Max made a frantic effort to set things right. "Ronny, no! I was lying! Nobody was hitting on Lorelei! I just had to get you to come to school!"

But Ronny Lugnitz in attack mode was impossible to call off. When Big heaved himself through the heavy exit door, Ronny was right on his tail, bellowing threats.

The dilemma almost tore Max in two. On the one hand there was the audience that he had been waiting for his entire life. On the other, there was Big, facing a shellacking at the hands of the toughest eighth grader in school. And it was all because of Max.

With a cry of, "I'll be back, okay?" he was off the stage and out the door.

Sydni was right behind him. "Max, are you *crazy*?"

"Wait up, guys!" called Maude. "I've got flat feet!" She joined the chase, barreling headlong into a sign painted on a pink bedsheet. As she plowed straight ahead, the banner snagged in her belt buckle, billowing behind her like Batman's cape: MAXX COWMEDY.

Behind them in the Giggle factory, an uneasy murmur and a few chuckles rippled through the audience.

"Don't worry!" called Mr. Lugnitz. "It's all part of the act! Show's not over—I hope."

Strung out in a line like the leaders in a marathon, the runners pounded across the parking lot and down the sidewalk—Big, Ronny, Max, Sydni, and Maude.

"Okay, Romeo!" howled Ronny. "Now you're gonna pay!"

Suddenly, a black streak darted up the street and fell in beside Big, matching his speed.

Even in his moment of peril, Big was glad to see the newcomer. "Darth! We're in trouble, man! How come you can never find a Death Star when you need one?"

The cat meowed sympathetically and kept pace.

A hulking SUV roared up beside them. The back window rolled down, and Amanda Locke stuck her head out.

"Darth! Come home! We've got Cat Yummies for you, sweetie!"

"Amanda, can I talk to you about something?" shrieked Sydni from twenty feet behind the car.

"Faster, Mom, faster!" Ninth grader Madison Locke appeared beside her sister. Her eyes fell on Maude, hop-skipping at the back of the pack as the brisk wind wrapped the banner around her legs. "Nice pants!"

Maybe it was a case of light-headedness brought on by sprinting in this procession. But Max couldn't shake the feeling that he was not part of the craziness, but watching from a distance. Comedians had to be observers, after all, to come up with good material.

All at once, he laughed out loud, and his labored strides became loose and easy. Sure, this was all completely nuts. But without insanity, where would the jokes come from?

And without jokes, how could you be the Funniest Kid in America?

Mr. Brown

". . . Thank you,
ladies and gentlemen!
You've been a great audience!
Good night!"